O F
O C E A N
A N D
A S H

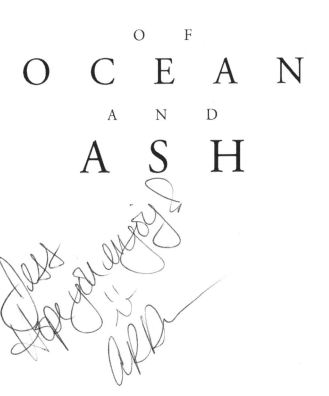

A. R. DRAEGER

DRAEGER

Of Ocean and Ash by A.R. Draeger
Copyright ©2015 Amber Draeger
www.amberdraeger.com

Cover designed by Staci, quirky-bird.com
Interior designed by Nadège, inkstainformatting.com
Editing by Allison, thewriteconclusion.com

Also available as an ebook.

Published in association with the Falling in Deep Collection.

For JOSH, my Hubbins.
I have now immortalized that nickname in print for all the
world to read. I love you with all my heart.

For MOM.
Sex scene is more graphic in this one than in the previous.
Beware, and don't say I didn't warn you.

To MARSHA.
May you find some light in those dark places.
In the meantime, put this book down. I'll write a clean one for
you someday.

O F

O C E A N

A N D

A S H

p r o l o g u e

SUMMER WAS WANING WHEN I was born, marked by the heat leaving the waters and the nights growing longer. My family wanted to migrate with the rest of their people, but they waited for me in the stillness of the waves, keeping an ever-watchful eye.

Mother heard the wails of the fisherman's wife the night the woman discovered she carried me in her womb. The fisherman and his wife lived next to the water in a small, dilapidated shack made of rotten wood and leaky thatch. They had six children before me, although Mother knew not in what mixture their genders numbered. All but two were taken away at birth. The couple had too many as it were for a meager fisherman and his wife, and I was yet another mouth to feed.

The fisherman's cries of mercy woke my family the night I was born. My arrival was sooner than expected, his wife not having carried me nine months in her womb. I was tiny, frail. My left leg was misshapen, my head oblong.

Mother watched him from beneath the surface, saw his tanned sailor's skin, ebony and white streaked hair, and grey-whiskered face. He looked down at me, the fragile bundle cradled in his arms, and cried out through parched lips and crooked, black teeth:

"Forgive me, O God! Have mercy on her. I leave her to your care."

He dropped me in the water with a small *plop*.

My sister, Liliana, caught me before I plunged too far into the depths. My family crowded around me, anxious and excited. My uncles debated eating me, seeing my size and stature, convinced I would not survive. Mother waved them off and took me from my sister's arms, cradling me as my still-human lips turned blue.

It was an enormous challenge for a human to come into the fold. Not many of us were capable of such a change, but Mother knew my lineage had been on and in the water. She had watched my father and his father before him.

She lowered her lips to my nose and mouth, and she breathed into me the life of the sea dwellers, the *merfolk*. I sputtered a bit, and my body shivered, unsure of the transformation. Mother held me tight, sang me lullabies of the whales, and when all my family had lost hope that I'd survive, I woke.

My scream was shrill, she said. Loud, piercing. She was proud, surprised at the pushing force of the water I had generated. She knew I would be a good Caller.

With that, they gathered to me – my mother, sister, uncles, aunts, and cousins – and in a ritual almost lost in the passage of time, sang as my mother fed me two drops of her blood.

My legs lengthened and molded together, as her nourishment pulsed through my body, changing me inch by inch. Where my feet had once been, two fins took shape, overlaid with iridescent blue scales.

The process was beautiful, my family told me, *rare*, and yet there I was, the adopted, healthy and changing. Born human, and through the grace and love of the one I would know as Mother, turned into a creature of the deep, a daughter of the ocean, a *mermaid*.

o n e

I RAN MY FINGERS THROUGH my hair, and the motion failed to ease my dissatisfaction. My locks had been cut short the day prior. The feel of the crude length in between my fingers disappointed me, and it always had.

Mother let it grow longer than she should, fascinated by my strands of gold.

"*Someday.*" I heard her whisper, holding to the hope that my voice would sound out soon. If it did, I would be a Caller, and there would be no more cutting. My hair would grow to a gorgeous length, and Mother would comb and braid it lovingly.

The Calling Days were filled with ritual. The beautiful braids would be loosened, combed through and shined with ground pearls. The mothers would whisper sacred words to the

Callers, and those sacred daughters would swim up until the light broke through the surface and beyond.

Only the Callers had long hair, and they were proud of it, some more prideful than they should be. Their lengthy tresses were beautiful, and they were enticing to the men they lured, they said, stroking their strands in front of us shorn Untried and Lessers.

Our clan had rarely more than seventeen Callers. My four sisters came into their positions early, each possessing the melodic, high-pitched voice of our now retired mother. They would have their own families soon, and the eldest of my sisters was already mated to the strongest male of our tribe.

Only I was left untested, and Mother grew more anxious with each season. I was rare, she said, me with my golden hair among the naturally dark-haired merfolk, and my large eyes the color of sea foam. My breasts were plump and hips wide to birth young.

Mother made a list of males for me, some of them with exceptional status among our kind, but I could only be mated if I were a Caller. The females without a voice were little more than servants – Lessers.

My family hadn't produced a Lesser in four generations. Then again, I was adopted. Once a human, pitied and turned. Some wagered against me, and even my own sisters held doubts, but never Mother. To her, I just needed more prodding and a little more time.

"Ia!"

I heard her voice a world away, could sense the excitement in it.

"Ia! Come here, now!"

I stopped fumbling through my crude hair, and gathering my composure, I swam in the direction of her voice, following the current and a few wayward schools of small fish, thinking that perhaps I should snack before I approached her.

She found me before I could give it a second thought.

"You are Calling."

My jaw slacked open. "Tonight?"

I had not been made aware I would be tested, had not been practicing as I should.

"Of course, child," a low voice from behind me answered, and I turned to face shining eyes highlighted by deep wrinkles at their corners. Our *High* Mother, Queen of not just our tribe, but our entire clan.

I stumbled over proper forms of address, instead choosing to lower my head to show some reverence. Her hand lifted my chin, and my gaze met hers.

"You have seen twenty-five years come late fall. That is close enough," the High Mother said, her eyes narrowing as she studied me.

"Mother, is this what you wish as well?" I asked, hoping for support in delaying this, but found only a sigh as a response. Mother seemed hesitant to answer me, pausing before she answered, and considered the gaze of the Queen in our midst as well as the looks of the people that were gathering around us.

The High Mother raised her eyebrows as she turned her attention to Mother. It was foolish to deny the High Mother.

"Two ships have been spotted," Mother replied to me. "You call, or you fail and the young mermen find another beauty to pine for. Our High Mother is right. You are of age, and it is time."

"Good," the High Mother said. "I was hoping for more interesting activities besides the usual mating ceremonies. A test is always full of excitement." She winked at me with a smile on her lips as she turned to leave with her entourage. "And surprises. Always *full* of surprises."

Mother bit her lip and clasped her hands in front of her as she turned to join the High Mother's entourage, then swam away, leaving my thoughts to chase the shrinking iridescent green of her fins. Chattering jolted me, and I found remnants of our voyeurs studying me, some haughty, certain of my failure, and others stressed. The faces of the Lessers were lined with worry.

No one who had truly lived life at the bottom ever wished it on others.

I did not cry, at least not where anyone would witness. I turned and fled in the direction opposite my mother, my tail flexing as fast as it could go, propelling me through the depths until the light grew incredibly dim.

I took refuge in a dark grotto, long abandoned by life. I had found it as a small child, fleeing the insults and jeering of my peers, and anytime I found my life overwhelming, my future forlorn, and my choices stolen, I retreated to my silent sanctuary.

This day was darker than others, and the entrance to the cave sat before me, a gloomy mouth opened wide. Instinct told me to leave, to seek my family, but I knew they would bring me no comfort. Tracing the ancient drawings of the humans along familiar walls always brought peace of mind to me, brought my thoughts to an arena of 'what-ifs'.

What had this place been, long ago, to the humans? It hadn't always been underwater. Humans cannot breathe as we can, nor do their eyes see through the dark depths.

I swam in, my eyes adjusting to the change in light, the faint glow of the depictions warming up the atmosphere around me. I wound my way around the sharp edges of the ceiling to my favorite spot, a deep area with figures chasing enormous land creatures, and even a drawing of fire, yet another mystery of my birth-world that I had never experienced and had only seen from afar.

What would it be like to be as I was born – *human*? From what I had seen, the people above the surface were free. They ran, and walked, and laughed on the beaches. Lovers entwined themselves under the stars. Surely, their days were filled with sunshine and love, and such a people would treasure each other, and there would be no Lessers among them - Would there be?

I questioned Mother about their world often, and her answers would always fall to the story of my birth, and how my father had chosen death for me, but I wished to believe that it was because a part of him knew my true family awaited me beneath the waters, a family that could mend my frail, human form.

The human body was a weak one, indeed. Those I feasted on were grotesque creatures, with rough beards, blackened teeth, and tough skin. Wide, fearful eyes, too. I would wonder if I would have been as they - rough, rotten, and fearful of my death. I would hold on longer to them than I should, studying them, watching their mouths open as they gasped for air and their eyes widen with the realization that I would not be saving them.

It was painful to sink my teeth in, to feel the life of them spurt forth and drain down my throat, but it was necessary, no matter how I longed to help them to the surface, and no matter the pity I held for a creature that I could have been. Survival, my mother named it. It was my survival as opposed to theirs.

Tonight, too, would determine my fate. It would cement my place in our tribe, in our clan, in our kind. Should I fail, I would serve and be one of the silent ones that looked on the young Untried with furrowed brow.

"You will succeed," the masculine voice next to me whispered, the movement of his words bubbling in my right ear as a strong finger played with a strand of my shortened hair.

Smooth, deep, and haunting, his voice made most of the females giggle and sigh.

It grated down my spine.

"Hello, Ro," I said, flat and irritated.

"So this is where you come to hide."

My hand jerked up and wiped away the water leaking from my eyes. I had been crying, and he'd seen me. I pushed away from the wall and floated back into an open space.

"I am more than capable of catching you," he said.

"Is that a threat or a poor attempt at seduction?"

He laughed, and the smirk he gave me was evidence of both.

He had been after me since I had grown into a young adult, my curves and breasts blossoming. Ro was quick to make his intentions known, and as the youngest, strongest guard of my clan, he would have his pick.

I had been flattered, taken by the handsome merman with that gleam of lust in his eyes. His words, his compliments, enveloped me. If only I'd call, then I would be mated, be *his* for the rest of our long lives.

It was a dream readily crushed when I found him thrusting against one of my tribe's unwilling Lessers.

Fattened by a grand feast, most were asleep when a small cry, quickly silenced, roused me. I left the safety of my sisters and swam around our grotto, curious. Turning the corner of an older structure inhabited by Ro's family, I saw them and stopped, frozen, clinging to the wall next to me.

I couldn't remember her name. Many Lessers lost their names when they assumed their positions and instead took the names of their family. She was a year or two older than me, a more recent Lesser, with vibrant, short red hair that was now grabbed up to the scalp, forcefully, in one of his hands. The other hand greedily squeezed her breasts.

9

Tears streamed down her face as he grunted and groaned, slamming against her, and the sand of the floor blew up with the twitches of their fins. Harder, quicker he moved, her face tightening in pain under him until his head threw back, and his mouth opened in an 'O'.

Gathering herself, she took the moment to escape from beneath him, feeling the slack in his grip.

He rebounded, caught her before she could move. "I'm not done with you."

His face darkened again, and the hand still holding her hair pushed her head down past his chest and abdomen. My hands balled up into fists, and I started to move toward them, determined to defend her as best I could. A hand grabbed my shoulder, stopping me before I could step from the shadows. It was my sister, Liliana. Her eyes were wide, and she shook her head as she held a finger to her lips to silence any intention I had of voicing my dissent. After a moment, she pulled me to her, and we fled, having stayed as long as we had only due to my state of shock. It was akin to watching a shark tear at the limbs of one too slow to flee their death.

I was unknowing in the ways of mating, let alone abused mating. It terrified me at first, the fear evident on my face each time he neared, much to his confusion.

Then I became infuriated, especially when I saw his abused Lesser, swollen with young, banished to the growing reef for the duration of her *situation*. It was shameful, hurtful when her matriarch passed judgement, and the Lesser said nothing, not a word for her own defense.

I opened my mouth, but words failed me too as the realization hit me that no one would believe her.

Or me.

Or both of us.

Charming Ro had set himself up as the ideal merman, the destined Premier Guard of our tribe, and perfect mate. His great-grandmother had been a High Mother – a Queen – and his mother and father were among the elite of our tribe. His ancestry alone afforded him far more reverence than he deserved. To insinuate he raped a forbidden, chaste Lesser, would have been laughable and insulting, and I knew it as truth in the depths of my being. I would've taken the same disbelieving position as everyone else had I not seen him. For the first time in my short life, I understood – in its entirety – what Lesser truly meant, and it shook me to the core.

I'd been the receiver of many a cruel act from not being mer-born, but even I was regarded as above the Lessers.

Now, here he was.

Ro. Half propositioning me. Half threatening. His face and posture screaming that he'd do the same to me as that poor Lesser if he could get away with it. He might even try here if I angered him enough.

I smeared a smile across my face. "I need to be alone, Ro."

He shrugged. "You are worried that you will fail."

"What is it to you if I do fail?"

He moved closer, pressing himself to me. "It would be in your best interest if you don't, but," he paused, choosing his words. "I have never been one for restrictions."

I glared at him, my thoughts returning to that horrible night.

"You know I saw you." It slipped out, and half of me hoped it would shake him up.

He shrugged again as though it were a casual comment, nothing serious in its implication.

"I thought as much. Your behavior, your sudden dislike of me. I suspected that might have been you, hiding behind that

11

corner," he leaned in, his lips tickling my earlobe. "Caller or Lesser, either way, you are mine. Do not forget that."

He grinned as he backed away from me.

I shuddered. "Why me? Why not one of my sisters, or one of the ones who adore you?"

His head cocked to the side as he considered it, searching for an answer.

"Why do you deny me?" Hurt crossed his face for a brief moment before that all-too-slippery sneer tugged at the corners of his mouth again. "It makes me crave you all the more. Good luck tonight, Land-born. I will see you after." He winked, the glow of his purple mer-eyes paling as he backed away, and then he swam off, leaving me alone with my thoughts.

He will not have me. If I am a Caller, then I shall choose someone else. If a Lesser… I'll leave. I'll be forgotten, Forsaken, but at least I will not be his.

My hands tightened into fists at my sides as I swam back home.

t w o

"HE SWIMS *STRONG*, ONE OF the fastest, and I have no doubt his sons will offer great protection as he has for his family." Mother's voice held excitement when speaking of Ro, her focus shifting back and forth between my sister and me.

"Ro does fight well," I was always careful to compliment Mother's choices when she started beaming about the formation of our own families, even more so when she made us listen to her.

Liliana rolled her eyes as she smiled. She was as beautiful as all mer-born and had been tested already, declared to be a mother as soon as she'd selected a mate. Her call was strong; she'd claimed two ships in her first year alone.

She was once the top choice for Ro's family. His mother had flattered her incessantly over her beauty and great talent, but much to everyone's surprise, Lili refused to select a mate, instead choosing to take her first season as a Caller to bring honor to our family. I had wondered in those days who she was holding her heart for, who she was waiting on, and often questioned why she never seized the opportunity to profess her love. Liliana kept her desires as silent as her opinions. Not even our mother could read her, and our sisters were unable to drag a word out of her.

It was a pleasant surprise to have her as my Call Giver – the one who would instruct me, and ultimately, test me. She smiled as she held my hand, encouraging me, but I could see the concern in her eyes too.

After all, voices were inherited.

We surfaced side-by-side, and I was lost in the light. Although the sun was sinking below the horizon, it was blinding and beautiful. Our kind surface so rarely when we are not Callers, and I remembered the relaxing warmth of the sun on one of our annual visits.

I kept my sight fixed on the descending sun, enjoying the heat from it on my shoulders and face, wishing I could've had the day up here. I could hear the other Callers surfacing at our backs, giving us some distance and a little privacy.

"We'll have to stay in deeper waters tonight," Lili's voice was soft, gentle, and high. It soared when she sang, and yet sounded like a small child's when she spoke.

I nodded in reply, still studying the sun in its waning majesty.

"We will have a storm tonight. A bad one."

She pointed to the north, where the sky was already blackening with ominous clouds. "The ships will be here soon."

I raised my eyebrows and tilted my head to the side, confused. I saw nothing but the shore in the far, far distance that looked to be enveloping the sun with each passing moment.

"I can hear them, Ia," she said. "You will too. It's a taught ability, and necessary for all Callers."

I lifted my hand out of the water, watching the droplets run down my skin, back toward their origin. "Do you think I have it in me?"

She looked away for a moment, surveying the other Callers that were surfacing. "I hope so, Ia. I would not wish being a Lesser on my worst enemy."

"I wasn't aware you had any," I smiled, half-heartedly.

She huffed a little, eying me with irritation. "You need to take this seriously, sister."

I looked down to the depths, unable to see our home and Mother.

"I will not be a Lesser, Lili." I refused to say more. She knew what was on my mind, and her mouth fell open.

Leaving.

Forsaken.

"You do not mean that, Ia."

I sighed, feeling the weight of the discussion on top of the mounting anxiety for my test. "I do, Lili. I would rather be a feast for sharks than be locked in servitude to the likes of Ro."

The name took her aback. She swam closer, those beautiful features of hers contorted with concern. "Why him?" She paused. "Why do you believe you'll be serving *him* as a Lesser?"

"He is determined, *absolutely determined*, to mate with someone in our family," I said. "He will be *our* family."

I felt the shudder roll through her, and could see the drop of her face as she acknowledged the truth in my words.

My mouth opened to ask her of her thoughts, but all I could push out was a syllable before she interrupted me, covering my mouth with her hand.

"Listen," she whispered, her gaze traveling to a far off place. "Do you hear them? The ships?"

My focus shifted to my ears, but all I could hear was the movement of the sea around us and my own heartbeat. Thunder

15

sounded, startling me, and my concentration went to the building storm ahead.

I shook my head.

She looked back to the other Callers who, visibly, were hearing the same signs as she. "Tonight, Ia shall call for us," she yelled to them. "It is the first of her tests."

"So may she call," they replied in unison.

"May Great Mother give Ia a voice with which to bless us, with life, that we may have life."

"May it be so," they replied.

She turned to me. "This is where it becomes dangerous. Are you ready, Ia?"

I nodded. *As ready as I will ever be.*

SHE TOOK MY HAND, AND we swam, keeping our upper bodies above the water as our tails propelled us, until the others were but spots in the distance behind us.

"Look! Do you see?" She pointed to the north, and there they were.

Three ships. One after the other, small but growing.

The sun had all but faded now, and the storm was nearer. Lightning lit the sky above us, threads of iridescence wrapping in and out of the encroaching gray and black.

The sight scared me, and I fought the instinct to dive back to the safety of our grotto.

Liliana's calm, determined presence strengthened me. "It is going to be difficult for your first test, but you must try," she spoke up over the rising howl of wind.

More experienced or talented Callers used such acts of nature to their advantage, their gifts allowing for an extra-ordinary, hypnotic tone and volume that stretched for kilometers, convincing the men on the ship that their voice would guide them to safe passage.

I felt the rising waves before I saw them, the currents shifting swiftly beneath us, and we bobbed with them in the water, attune to the movement.

The ships were not as lucky. They were large, cumbersome, and the bulk of them rode the waves crudely, sometimes airborne for a moment before the bow crashed down, splashing violently into the next wave. The sails, radiant white in the fading light, teetered and tottered from side to side, the weight of them dragging the vessels down to a perilous distance.

Forms moved about on the deck, frantic, but calculated. Some pulled at ropes; others shimmied up to great heights. As their vessels neared, their shouts and commands could be heard softly in the winds.

"We must get closer," Liliana yelled, her voice dampened by the gale. "See the ship to the right? That is the leader."

She pointed, and I nodded.

The rain felt sharp as it fell, increasing from drops here and there to a barrage.

"I have to call over all this noise?"

"Yes!" She dove under, taking my hand.

We stared at each other for a moment as our eyes adjusted to the dark, and I knew from the look on her face that the weather was worrisome.

"Ia, we *can* decline this one. There will be other ships, and you have two attempts left."

I considered it. "Can you call through this?" I asked, the root of me knowing her answer as I pointed to the storm raging above us.

Liliana nodded.

"Maybe I should try," I thought out loud. "I would hate to discard this attempt without trying."

"Are you sure?" She took my other hand as she searched my face with her eyes.

"We will have to get ourselves as close as possible, and stay on the surface to lure them to the rocks," she said. "The others will join us when we get close, but it will be on you."

"Or you," I added, anticipating my failure.

The belly of the foremost ship approached, its shadow looming ever closer, parts dipping in and out of the view beneath the waves. I took a deep breath, the gills under my ears flexing and reveling in the reprieve of the saltwater, and then swam toward it, Liliana in tow.

"Surface......NOW," she shouted, and we both propelled up and through the water, jumping out of it from the force of our tails.

The ship was massive, the wood creaked and groaned even though it was soaked. I braced myself against its side.

"Now, *call*. When you have their attention, they will follow your voice," she yelled. "Start small and easy. Use a single, wordless tone."

I pulled air into my lungs, felt the pressure of it tingle and burn, and turned my head upward trying to direct my mouth to the edge of the deck as we bounded in and out of the storm-tossed sea. I parted my lips and let loose with all my strength, concentrating on trying to create the beautiful sound my family was known for.

Nothing came out save a deep, pebble-filled screech.

Liliana lost her grip on the side of the ship as her hands instinctively covered her ears, and she fell back into the depths, wincing as her eyes broke contact with mine.

The ship's movement grew more erratic by the second as the winds unleashed on us, and I too, lost my grip and retreated underwater. The waters beneath were angry as well. Their currents reached deeper and lifted the contents of the upper levels of the sea to the surface in towering waves.

Liliana screamed my name. I heard that much among the turmoil, but little else, and I followed her voice.

"We are in grave danger. This storm is more than either of us can handle, and the ships are -"

A large hull, like a giant beast, tore through the water as we were pulled up.

"Lili!" I cried out, watching my sister slam against the wood and bounce into darkness.

Pieces of wood skewered my vision; the roar of the winds and rain and crash stunned my hearing.

The humans screamed, some of them now overboard and floating helplessly in the waters with me. The ones still conscious gasped for breath, reaching their arms upward, straining for help, but found none as we were tossed about.

I strained to push myself deeper, knowing if I could make it past this pull, I could retreat to calmer waters and maybe find Liliana, but as I orientated myself, hard wood grazed the right side of my tail. Thrusting my fin up and down as fast as it would let me, I was determined to push away from the behemoth chasing me. Something sharp bit into my fin as the waters began to pull us all upward yet again. It tugged me back, and when I glanced back, I saw its reflective sheen.

A hook.

A very large hook.

The pain of it tore through me, and the desperation to free myself transformed into pure panic as I felt rough threads wrap around my tail, moving farther up my body, wrapping itself around my arms until I could no longer fight it. It was a net, and I was completely, utterly snared.

The ship plunged downward again, and I, tied mercilessly to its side, went with it, the force of it throttling me against the unyielding wood.

My vision darkened as my head grew light, and an unnatural deep sleep consumed me.

three

THE WEIGHT OF THE WORLD was on my body, or so it felt.

Pressure.

Enormous pressure in my head, in my ears.

Heat.

It bathed my skin, but it was not a comforting warmth. It was torturous, as though a thousand sharp rocks were scraping across every bit of me.

I coughed and knew from the pain of the water bubbling up my throat that I was no longer in the ocean.

Sand was beneath me, hot and gritty. I closed my fingers around it, cradling it. How different. It felt barely moist.

The light blinded me as I opened my eyes. Overwhelmed, I wiped the remnant of vile moisture from my lips with the back of my hand, noticing the red tint of my skin. Bright pink and burning, it felt it could rip with any movement.

How am I alive?

While merfolk may stay above surface as much as we like, our ability to breathe air is limited. Our human-like lungs are quickly exhausted to the point that we must return beneath the waters at least every other hour or so to draw in better breath through our gills. I suspected from the height of the sun that I had been here more than a few hours, perhaps even a day. The pain coursing through my body told me that I must make it back to the water.

Lifting myself up onto my elbows brought forth a new agony, the hooks and net digging in to the parts of me still entrapped. I released what barbs I could from my arms using my free hand and began to slide down the netting. Rolling on to my stomach would be painful but necessary if I were to dig the remaining hooks out of my tail. The ones in my back would have to remain there until I could make it home. The net I would have to carry, and hope against hope it would not snare something else or trap me along the way.

I groaned as I turned myself over, using the little strength in my arms that I had left. My tail was not cooperating. It convulsed as I tried to use it to assist my movement, and it jerked in multiple directions. I kept my eyes closed as I pushed myself up to sit, afraid of viewing the incredible damage that it suffered.

It might render me unable to swim, unable to survive, and cast me into a long and drawn out death on an unfamiliar beach.

I opened my eyes to find feet at the end of my tail, still bound with the netting and hooks. Not a tail at all.

Legs.

Two of them, with two feet at the end. I followed the reddened, angry skin, sliding my palms up it, my hands in as much disbelief as my eyes. They were mine, the legs. I stopped at my stomach, knowing from the ache of the sunburn and the shocks of pain from the still-embedded hooks that this was neither a dream nor an afterlife.

I had turned human, someway, somehow in the mess.

I sobbed, terrified of what lay before me. Legs. Feet. Hooks, nets, scrapes, scratches, gashes, bruises.

How do I get back my tail? How do I get home?

Legs. I had legs, but my left one was turned inward, the knee dislodged and bulging.

I reached behind my ears and grasped for gills that were no longer there. I wrapped my arms around me, seeking to find some comfort, some calm in the emotions flooding me.

Not only was I human, I was maimed.

Human.

The story of my birth, of my turning, rushed back to me. I was human, now, but not beautiful as the mermaid I had become. I was the human that I would have been had I lived.

The unwanted, deformed, weak human that her father threw to the depths of the ocean.

Then again, while my form was perfect in the water, I had failed my first test. The odds were growing that I would be a Lesser. Perhaps this weaker, human form was a gift. I took deep breaths to calm the turmoil within me, and studied my skin for a moment, watching as it crinkled then grew taut with my movement.

"Miss? Are you alive?"

It was a woman's voice. A human voice, soft, calm, and comforting.

She spoke English, but in an accent I had never heard. I took a moment before I responded, my head and body still reeling from the pain…and the surprise that I was still alive.

"I do not know." The words were difficult to say as my lips splintered and cracked. "How long have I been here on shore?"

"All day, I think. We have one other survivor that I know of, and he is not expected to live much longer." She kneeled down next to me, her face but a blur, and offered me water from a thick, leather pouch.

"We searched for survivors this morning. I am sorry we overlooked you. You are hurt bad, and I will take you to be healed, yes?"

I focused my sight on the sturdy, large frame next to me, and the details grew clearer with each second. Her skin was dark as midnight, smooth and rich, contrasted against the solid white dress she wore. The same cloth was wrapped about her head, just a tuft of soft brown hair peeking out at the top. Her eyes were kind, and her half-toothless smile, along with the gentle lines that framed it, told me she was loving, and I would be safe by her hands.

I took the offered water, and then gagged at the flavor. It was salt-less – something I had never tasted, but I knew the pain in my stomach signaled that I needed it. She pulled the sack of water back some.

"Easy, miss. You will be sick if you drink too much."

I nodded, keeping my grasp on the vessel as she draped a piece of fabric around me.

"Zatia lives not too far from here. She is a freewoman, a healer. She can give you clothes, too."

Clothes. Yes, many humans wear fabric about them, and I'll have to be one of them.

"Yes, that would be good." I replied, still unsure of my surroundings, but as I was at a loss for other options, I agreed to go.

The woman's stout muscles helped me to my feet, and I cratered.

"I will carry you. You are light." Without permission or protest, she swept my legs out from under my body and lifted, carrying me as one would an infant.

"What is your name, miss?"

"Ia."

She paused for a moment, glancing down at me before we continued on. "Eye-uh," she repeated. "I am Jiba."

Unsure of my response, I chose silence. Her name was as unique to me as mine was to her.

JIBA MOVED AT A QUICK pace. Sweat streaked down her face, and her breaths became more shallow and frequent as she, no doubt, pushed her stamina to its limit with the added burden of my weight.

Fields and a few houses loomed in the far distance when we reached a modest home. It appeared new, the wood in excellent condition compared to the rotten, aged shacks with brittle thatch on the dock that we'd settled near in the north. This structure was one story, simple, painted white. It was unassuming aside from the smear of red that stained the doorframe.

Jiba carried me up its cobblestone walkway, pausing halfway through to take a brief respite. She muttered something beneath her breath then continued her course. We were greeted by an open door.

A girl stood behind it, slumping in that awkward limbo between youth and womanhood, the soft pink of her palms grasping the edge. She shrunk from view as best she could, seeking cover in the shadow as she searched me with her small, inquisitive eyes, and then turned away when they met my gaze.

"Nattie," Jiba spoke to her, her voice smooth and slow as she carried me inside. "Close the door behind me."

A heavy sigh heaved from the girl's chest as she pushed it to, the shadow of the door receding and revealing her petite form and night-kissed skin.

"Zatia won't like this, mama," Nattie's frail voice whispered on the wind away from us, her speech less accented than her mother's.

"I won't like what, girl," called a heavy, sultry voice from the back of the house. Jiba carried me farther in, following the voice and a strange aroma that began to waft through the house.

"A woman from the shipwreck," Jiba called out to the disembodied voice.

"Matthias told you to bring all survivors to the estate grounds. Master's orders," the woman said as pots and pans clanked about.

"She is hurt." Jiba called out over the clanging, and it ceased for a moment.

"Fine," the voice replied, and Jiba turned us to face a door next to the main entrance. It was worn, more so than the rest of the house as far as I could see. A large red dot was painted in the middle.

Nattie opened it without a word, her lips moving quickly to mouth an unspoken prayer.

The room was small, cluttered, and archaic compared to the structure that contained it. Dirt was dusted on the floor; plants grew next to every window with stalks bent to the light, drinking in the sun. Dried leaves hung from the ceiling, forming a canopy.

Jiba laid me down on the floor in the center of a giant circle of white that smelled of salt. Her rough, calloused hands lifted my head and placed a small bundling of straw beneath it to cushion me.

Every bit of my body ached.

The door opened, and in walked the commander of the house, the owner of the hoarse, low voice. The sunlight pouring in from the windows illuminated her smooth ebony skin. She pursed her plush lips as she crossed her arms and examined me with her golden-brown eyes. She was beautiful. Breathtaking. Her features bold yet delicate. Her age was only hinted at when she leaned close to me, and I saw soft wrinkles forming at the outer corners of her eyes.

"Pale for a slave, for someone who does hard work in the sun." Her words were sardonic, yet true. Jiba smirked, and looked up at her.

"She is new, from the north. Maybe she works in the house," Jiba reasoned.

Zatia shrugged, waving off Jiba's explanations. "He will be angry that you have brought a white woman here, Jiba," Zatia's voice was even-keeled with a tinge of scolding. She raised her eyebrows as she addressed her counterpart.

"Will you help her or not?" Jiba stated. "Her leg is bad."

Zatia grunted as she took my right foot in hand and reached with the other into a leather apron draped around her neck, pulling out a tool, metallic and worn.

"Have to get these barbs out," she said, showing me the tips of the pliers. "It will be very, very painful. I will work as quick as I can, yes?"

I nodded, breathing out through my nose as the tip of the tool dug into the holes of my flesh. A quick jerk of Zatia's arm freed broken fragments of the hooks that had snared me.

Pain ripped through my body, and tears formed in my eyes. Jiba leaned close, cradling my head, and began to sing a soft song.

Zatia paused.

"She was born like this," she said to Jiba, her tone easing off its earlier abrasiveness. "Her knee, the bone, all of it. Nothing I can do but mend where the barbs tore."

I looked down at my legs again. My left was mangled indeed. The knee bent inward toward my right side at an awkward angle. An equally deformed musculature restricted its movement. My left foot pointed in to the right as well, and down, the calf that controlled it in a permanent flex.

Zatia pressed her hand softly against my forehead. "You rest as best you can."

With a snap of Zatia's fingers, Nattie appeared with a pitcher of water in one hand and torn rags in the other. She knelt next to Zatia and me, dipped the rags in the water and scrubbed off the matted dirt and blood as Zatia continued her work, yanking barbs free from my skin and muscles.

The water was warm, soothing.

"Thank you," I said, and the women paused to look up at each other before resuming their work, a gleam of surprise in their expressions.

"You are welcome," Jiba replied, smiling as she took my hand in hers. "You are in good hands. I must get back to work. I will return, and if you are well enough, I'll take you to the main house."

I nodded, muscle spasms ripping through my concentration with each of Zatia's maneuvers.

Nattie followed her mother out; her high-pitched voice carried through the door despite its low volume. She returned with a smile, more at ease with my presence, and continued her task of cleaning me up.

"What is your name?" Zatia's voice cut through the silence.

"My people call me Ia," I replied.

Her hands halted for a second, considering the name. "Where are you from?"

The answers churned in my mind for a moment. Should I tell her the truth? That I come from deep under the waves?

That I feed on her kind?

Do I lie to these women who have saved me?

"I'm from the north," I said, hoping that it was sufficient enough to quell the questioning for now.

"You were lucky Jiba found you." She stood, wiping bloody hands on her apron. "The others would have done as they were told and dragged you to work as you were."

"Will she be punished because of me?"

Zatia sighed as she dug through the herbs hanging over our heads, pulled leaves off here and there, and then crumbled them in her fist. "Perhaps, perhaps not. It is of no matter. Jiba chose her course," Zatia said. "She is a gentle spirit, strong, but even she can be broken. You best not tell anyone that she brought you here."

She knelt over me, caressing my face in her hands. "Especially my son," she continued, her lips and jaw tensing. "Lie. Say you did not know the face, and they left you on the doorstep."

I nodded, and she spoke in her native language to Nattie, who fetched another pitcher of water.

"I must close your wounds, but first, we must clean them. It may hurt."

I again nodded, this time, closing my eyes and bracing myself for more pain. The warmth of the water trickled from the cloth onto a spot of raw, rent tissue. It was salt water. *Ocean* water. Heated, and comforting. I felt my body soaking it in, consuming it, thirsty for it.

A small gasp escaped Zatia, and I opened my eyes to find her staring at my legs. The areas touched by the saltwater were glowing, ever so slightly transforming red, angry tears into pink ones, sealing the skin up around them until my flesh became as new.

Nattie froze, mouth agape. Zatia looked down at me, eyes wide and eyebrows raised. "What are you, Ia?"

The words came out slowly, softly.

I parted my lips to tell her the truth of my origin when the door burst wide open, slamming into the wall adjacent.

"You were warned not to bring white people here."

A deep, angry voice resounded in my ears. The voice was an English one, with but a hint of the unusual accent I'd been hearing.

The man was tall, the hat on his head almost touching the top of the door frame. His skin was a light brown with gold like the deeper clay from the northern shores, and his lips were plush, his cheekbones high and sculpted. The wide-brimmed hat he wore concealed wavy black hair, or so I could tell from the wayward strands that peeked out.

But it was his eyes that captured me. Vibrant, light green made absolutely radiant by the dark contrast of his skin. Angry, yes, enraged even, but my, they were *beautiful*. Unlike any human's I had seen before, unlike the weathered, aged, rotten-toothed sailors we feasted on.

He stepped in as Zatia stood, and she and Nattie both kept their heads and sight directed to the ground as Zatia tossed a tattered cloth over me to shield my nakedness from his sight.

"Defy me again, and I cannot save you from the trouble he'll bring on you. Understand me?"

Zatia and Nattie both nodded, their hands clasped solemnly in front of them.

"Take her," he ordered.

An African man stepped around him, sliding in between him and the door. He wore only a pair of pants, white and marred with stains, kept up by rope at his waist. His eyes never met mine.

He kneeled next to me and lifted, but unlike the gentle carriage of Jiba earlier, he threw me across his shoulder, and I found myself looking at the ground, an uncomfortable pressure growing where my stomach met the bones of his shoulder.

The sun outside blinded me again, and I jerked in surprise as the man tossed me into a small wagon. My back slammed against the wood, but I did not cry out.

"Sorry," the man spoke, but his words were muffled, full of weight. As he turned to leave, I noticed both of his ears were swollen shut, the lobes ballooned and twisted. Scar upon scar streaked across his back, highlighted by glistening sweat. Some of the skin still held a pinkish hue as though it lingered in a constant state of healing.

"He said, 'sorry'. He's half-deaf, he is. Beaten until his ears were done for, or so it looks, probably by the previous owner. You'll come to understand him in time. Here. Put this on," a feminine voice spoke from behind me she draped another cloth around my shoulders. "You are very lucky to have lived. Very few have made it."

I glanced back to find a hefty, pale, pinkish woman smiling at me from the driver's bench.

"You'll have to forgive me, dear. I'm Mary." She giggled. "I serve in the kitchen. Followed my husband over, I did. He's a cook." She extended a hand.

I took it, following her lead.

"When I heard that someone lived through that awful mess, and it was a woman, and you were...well, like me, I thought I'd tag along with Mr. Matthias to come fetch you," she continued, words flying out faster than I could perceive them.

The driver, the very same man who unloaded me, climbed up next to Mary and took the reins. He called out with a strong, slurred voice to the horse latched to the wagon, and we jolted forward, almost sending me sprawling. Mary caught me by my shoulders.

"Oh, you poor thing. You must be horribly frightened and exhausted. We'll have you fixed up in no time."

Her face was kind, excited even, but as I glanced at the driver's ears and scarred back, I could not shake the feeling that I was being carried into a world far more dangerous than I'd imagined. Mary poured out her every thought, her history, the years she and her husband would work for land and freedom, the night's menu, where I would likely be stationed considering my unfortunate disability.

All of it flowed through my mind for a fleeting moment, every other thought urging me to make my way back to the water, to my people, to my healed, underwater body.

I sat silent, half-listening to Mary as we traveled for some distance, our wagon clicking by field after field of a tall crop, the green of it washed out by the light of the afternoon sun. Sweat-drenched slaves toiled in the heat. Younger girls and older women hauled water in buckets, giving each worker a ladleful at a time. The cracks of whips cut through the air, followed by the pent-up wails of some of the poor souls on the receiving end.

The man who burst into Zatia's home rode alongside the cart.

I felt his stare on me, studying my misshapen form.

He said nothing as he stretched his back in the saddle, rotating his left shoulder. I met his gaze for a moment then looked down at the passing ground.

"Three ships, twelve survivors, most too broken to work, and then we have this one," he continued with a nod toward me. "Of all the able-bodied on board, this mangled one is the one who lived." He sighed.

"Can't work the fields, at least, not well. Plenty of servants and slaves in the house. God, I pray you are not my responsibility. I wouldn't know where to place you. Who do you belong to, girl?"

I looked up at him, confused by the question, and felt the heat as my face flushed with anger.

"Are you deaf and dumb as well? Your contract. Who owns you," he raised his voice, slowed his words.

"Oh, come, Matthias. Really, must you badger the girl," Mary pleaded with him, half-scolding. "I'm sure we'll get a full account of everything once she's had a good meal and rest. She may not know who she is to go to. She may not can read, for Christ's sake."

"If she's not Lord Malcom's property, then she's not my concern," Matthias stated.

"God have mercy, Matthias," she shook her head. "I'll tend to her until you and the Master sort it out. Don't you worry none over her. You'll probably never even see the likes of her again."

Matthias leaned back, slacking, studying us with that stern gaze. Angered by his embittered tone toward me, I kept my sight on him, refusing to look away as he assessed me with his eyes yet again. He turned his attention back to the road ahead, clicking his tongue as he spurred his steed onward.

"That's Matthias. He's the foreman, overseer of all of us," she said, lowering her voice. "And believe it or not, he's the most lenient. The others are nasty, *nasty* men. Matthias is harsh with all of us, but he has to be. If he isn't, Lord Malcom will put someone else in his place, and God knows they'd be rotten," she paused for a moment, weighing her words. "He wasn't always the cruel man you see today. Circumstance has made him that way."

Mary's voice was apologetic, and the sympathy she held for him shone in her eyes, but I could not dismiss his insulting manner. I knew nothing of the man as he knew nothing of me, and he had already deemed me worthless. Unfit for even menial tasks.

I heard the fisherman that sired me, or what I imagined he would have sounded like, in Matthias' voice, in Matthias' opinion, and knew without a doubt that he was a danger to me. After all, the fisherman drowned me at birth.

I had no words to respond to Mary's attempt at easing my anger. Instead, I nodded and turned my attention back to the ground.

Earth. Something I never imagined I'd walk on. Terrifying and exhilarating. I could catch a glimpse of what life might have been for me - develop an understanding of the creatures that kept us alive. Maybe, even, find a way to learn something, *anything*, to take back to my tribe and make me worth a little more than they would determine me otherwise.

My thoughts flashed to my Calling test. The pit of my stomach told me I was most likely not a Caller, but this experience on land might be enough to keep my same station above the Lessers.

Ro's voice floated through my mind, and sent shivers down my spine.

And then the thought struck me. *What if this is permanent? What if I am destined to spend the rest of my existence onshore?* I would not know the answer until I could step back into the waters that threw me out, of that I was completely sure.

Lost in thought, I failed to notice the coolness of the shade stretching over us until we passed through a large, finely crafted stone arch. It was unlike anything I had seen, smooth and delicate. We were under trees for a short distance, winding our way along a more gentle path than the one previously traveled. The trees opened up, and there, at the end of the way, stood an enormous structure.

Living in the waters limited my view to huts and buildings next to docks, and I was awed by the monstrous estate before me.

"Ah, she is beautiful, isn't she? Melina Hills is what they call her. I've seen larger and finer estates back home, of course, but for here, she's a palace fit for a king."

Mary smiled at my expression, giving me a few moments to take it in.

"Weren't expecting something this fine here, were you?"

I shook my head. The manor stretched tall and mighty, four rows of windows indicating different floors. The bottom of the house was cut into the land; smaller windows adorned it. The craftsmanship on the stonework and façade grew more evident as we neared, high arches accented each doorway, smaller ones embellished the windows, and a giant balcony extended from the third floor, giant columns stretching down to the ground supporting it.

"That, of course, is the main house," she nodded to the giant residence before us. "We, my husband and I, live just off the main house with some of the other house servants. That's where you'll be, too, if this is where you're contracted."

She eyed me up for a second, hoping for a sign of confirmation, but I kept my focus on the sprawling complex before me as she continued. "There aren't many of we Irish here anymore. The blacks outnumber us by far. The slaves quarters are a ways off, back toward the hill to the right, see? Closest to the fields."

It was then I noticed we were surrounded by hills, tall ones that stretched toward the sun and rolled off toward the horizon.

"We're in a nice spot, indeed. High winds tear though quite a bit, with it being an island and all, but little damage here. Protected," she smiled as we wound our way to the back of the building. The driver slowed the cart to a stop, and Mary stood as he walked around to help us out the back.

I looked around, awestruck, as he lifted me out of the cart and waited as I stretched my legs, placing my feet on the ground. My knees trembled beneath me, having never been used, and I began to cave in on my own self. He caught me, tenderly held me up upright – a stark contrast to his earlier manner.

"Thank you," I said, watching as his eyes studied the movement of my lips. A small smile touched his lips, revealing blackened, broken, and missing teeth. From the scars on his back and the swell of his ears, I knew this man had a harder life than I could ever imagine, and my heart pained for him.

"Haven't your land legs yet, have you?" Mary commented, giving a gentle tug to the driver's arm toward the house. He turned to watch her.

"Best help her in, Asa, then report back to Mr. Matthias."

The man nodded, and swept my legs upward, cradling me as he carried me through a large wooden door, held open by Mary.

f o u r

DESPITE THE HEAT, THE HOUSE was cool. Every window in sight was ajar, welcoming a warm but stirring breeze. Large draperies moved in the wind, and I marveled at the finery around me.

I had seen such fabrics before. My people insisted on grabbing what we could from the sinking ships, sometimes stumbling on things we'd never seen, more so to teach us the ways of our prey than anything else.

Every once in a great while, a female would be on board, wrapped in such exotic finery that it would scare some of the younger, more unfamiliar ones away from feeding. The like of her was indeed rare, but beautiful and utterly mesmerizing. The fabric floated about her, lifting toward the surface, and yet she continued to sink. The light would catch the cloth, and I would marvel in the beauty of it, the colors, the texture. Some of the fish of the southern waters had colors such as those.

And here some of that regalia was, used in plentiful bounty for decoration.

Mary walked in front of us, leading the way down the hall and into a great chamber that stood, to me, as tall as the sky. Light danced on the floor in an array of wonderful color from the glass that hung from the ceiling.

Asa paused there, and we waited as Mary approached an older man who seemed to stand guard at the bottom of an enormous staircase. He was dressed in finer clothes than the lot of us. Of course, any and all of this was completely new to me, let alone the words to describe them. My mouth remained agape, closing only when the gentleman showed us into what I would come to know as a parlor.

Asa again paused, but this time, stooped to lower me down to an ornate, gilded chair. The gentleman saw this and immediately approached us with waving gloved hands, making us aware that we were not welcome to touch a thing.

A few moments passed before Mary reappeared, motioning for us to enter through a smaller door opposite us. Asa, having resituated me in his grip, hesitated for a breath, then did as she directed.

Dark wood covered most of the walls save one, which was lined with shelf after shelf of books. The room was ill-lighted compared to what I had previously experienced, and it took me a minute to notice two me at the far end of the room. One was seated behind a large desk, and Matthias stood before him.

Their voices were hushed, but heated, and as we neared, I could make out some of the conversation.

"Deaf, dumb, crippled, she'd be of no use here," the seated one stated, his clothing much like the draperies and fabric adorning the house. Clean and crisp, his attire was a stark contrast to Matthias' simple clothes. "She'd be another mouth to feed and for what?"

Matthias stood erect, silent, everything about his carriage showing his reverence for the man – undoubtedly the master of this estate.

The man behind the desk pursed his lips, swirled around a brandy-filled glass. His voice was just above a whisper.

"The facts are thus: I have checked our records and found no such listing of a *maimed* female servant, although it may be that one of our newer neighbors may be seeking house servants of a paler complexion. I have sent word across the island and will do so to the harbor master of the closest islands," He paused, taking a sip of his drink. "Considering her condition, the odds are high that an able-bodied member of her family signed the agreement, and she took said kin's place."

The master leaned forward, taking a quill and piece of parchment in hand.

"If her contract is not located and ownership of contract remains unknown, we will address her station then. In the meantime," the man continued. "You will find her work here in exchange for food and shelter. *If* she proves useless, we will sell her debt and contract her to someone else."

Matthias sighed, perhaps of relief or perhaps a sign of the burden he would now carry.

"Yes, sir."

"And Matthias," the man replied. "You will not allow *Christian* peoples: slaves, servants, or otherwise, to be *healed* by your mother. God forbid anyone of consequence receives word of it. You may visit her at will, but you will not allow a repeat of today's actions."

"Yes, sir."

The man nodded, satisfied that Matthias would heed him, and then he took notice of our presence.

"Ah! And here is the subject of our excitement."

Asa straightened as best he could while holding me, tension shooting through his muscles as the man walked around his desk and over to us.

"Matthias, you did not tell me she was beautiful," he said, never taking his eyes off of me. They were green, a mirror of Matthias', but there was something in his manner that made me feel as if I were a banquet to be devoured.

Matthias' face paled as the master of the house studied me. His strong, wide shoulders slumped slightly as he watched us, and he ran his fingers along the brim of the hat he was holding.

"You have been through quite the ordeal, young lady."

He gazed down his nose at me, taking stock of my form and condition. He snapped his fingers, and Matthias strode to us, peering over the master's right shoulder.

"Sir?"

"See to it that she is fed, and find her suitable sleeping quarters. Place her with the house servants," he said. "And for God's sake, find some appropriate clothing for her." He kept his sight on me the entire time, never once turning Matthias' direction. His tongue brushed his bottom lip.

Matthias vanished as quickly as he had appeared, his quickening footsteps the only indication he was still in the room.

"What is your name, girl?" The man asked.

"Ia," I answered, my voice hoarse and low.

The master's brow furrowed. "Ia," he spoke, rolling my name on his tongue. "So, you are neither deaf nor mute. And you are from Ireland, yes?"

"From the north," I said.

The man shrugged and turned his back to me, working his way to the throne-like chair behind his desk.

"Your manner of speaking is odd, even for an Irishwoman," the man said, matter-of-factly. "I suppose that may be another issue of your...condition? I am not familiar with much of Ireland. My family holds lands in the Scottish highlands." The man sat down and began to scribble in a large ledger.

"I am Lord Malcom, originally suited to a much finer life in England, although this has been my home for some years, thanks in part to the poor governance of my predecessor," he said, half of his words either mumbled or tainted with a slight slur.

"You will address me as my title demands, and you will work for room and board here."

He peered over his nose at me again, and I nodded.

"You must understand that I am overly kind. Many would have left you to rot on that beach," he continued, scribbling more on the document in front of him. "I am so kind as to provide you with food, clothing, and a place to sleep, as well as the opportunity to work to repay the debt."

He sat down the quill, this time tapping a finger on the desk as his brow furrowed. "I will not remind you again of your place. Address me accordingly, and with respect to my station, as well as with the awareness of yours, yes?"

I nodded, but could see a newly returned Matthias in the background mouthing, "Yes, sir" to me.

"Yes, Lord Malcom, sir."

Lord Malcom's face softened, and he waved us away. Asa was quick to reply with a nod of recognition as he turned to carry me out. The exit opened before us, revealing the quiet, silver-headed gentleman who saw us in. He led us a different way than we had entered, taking us through narrow corridors until he opened another door, and the sunlight blinded us.

WE WALKED IN SILENCE, ASA carrying me, and Matthias next to us. Facing his direction, I studied him as he stared straight ahead, the shadow of his hat shading most of his face.

"You are Zatia's son, aren't you?" I asked, hoping that a touch of conversation would lighten the tension. Already awkward and unsure of myself in this strange place, I believed myself to have little to lose.

He stopped, and Asa halted with him.

"I am," he said, "and you will not ask questions of me nor will you say anything of my mother, or I will toss you to *them*." He nodded in the direction of the fields, some distance away. I could see a white overseer pacing back and forth, yelling at those working the soil.

"Understand?" Matthias asked as he motioned to Asa for us to continue moving.

"You are in charge of them," I commented.

"Barely," he said, sighing. "That's none of your concern."

"It weighs heavy on you?"

Matthias stopped again, this time casting me a glance filled with hurt and curiosity. A long breath filled his lungs. "Yes."

He turned to open the narrow wooden door of the long, white building before us.

"Why are you helping me?" I asked. After all, he could have left me to his overseers as he had threatened.

"My mother asked me to," he said as he prepared to shut the door, Asa and I having already entered the dark corridor.

"Thank you," I replied, and his tense, hardened features softened for an instant before the door slammed shut between us.

f i v e

I WAS AT THE FAR end of a sizeable room. The beds were nothing more than hay and cloth on the floor. The grottos I had called home were far more comfortable and luxurious to me than these cramped quarters. I would share them with multiple other women, pale and dark alike, but all of them members of the house ranks.

A small group came to see what the fuss was about and meet the survivor of the shipwreck. One of the women laughed when I explained my confusion at the division of the living quarters. I had seen many women in the fields on the way to the main house.

They explained that the field slaves had separate quarters away from our own. We were not to intermingle, or so I was warned, unless we wanted to join them. We were not to intermingle with males of our own kind either, a robust, redheaded woman also warned. She made it evident there would be no difficulties on my part, however, hinting at my leg with a wave of her hand.

"More a formality to tell you," she said. Her name was Rose, but as there were three other Roses in the same sleeping quarters, she answered to Ann. She tended to the laundry, the clothes of the Master and his folk, as well as all the white servants, as few as they were.

"What of Matthias? Is it permissible to speak to him?" I asked, praying that I would not be barred from speaking with one of the few individuals that I had been acquainted with, regardless of his malcontent.

The women looked to each other, and I could tell from their glances they were choosing their words.

"He's a handsome one, he is," one of the younger ladies said, batting her eyes.

"Oh, get off it," a crass, gray-headed woman wiped her wrinkled brow. That was the second Rose, but as the oldest, she kept her name.

"You treat him as his position commands, but you remember – he ain't but a smidgen above you." She spoke as though the mere mention of him put bile in her mouth, and she could not spit him out fast enough.

They chatted for a considerable while before the elder Rose reminded the whole of them that the last of their daily duties were waiting, as well as supper. She invited me to work alongside her, cleaning, once I got around, but was careful to do so only after the others began making their way down the hall, a small hint of pity in her eyes.

And so I sat, using the moments of silence to allow the reality of my situation to sink in, when Mary entered, determined to have me walk about.

"The more you rest on it, the worse it will be. I know these things." She smiled as she stood in front of me. "I'm going to wrap my arms around your waist, and on the count of three, you are going to push up. And don't you worry none, I am a stout woman."

She didn't wait for a reply.

"Three," she shouted with a grunt as she lifted. I used what strength I had to comply, and the sudden throw of weight caught her off-guard, sending her backward toward the sole mirror in the room.

Catching our balance within inches of striking the looking glass, we shuffled our way to the broomstick resting in the corner next to my bed. Mary loosened her hold on me, and I grew more confident in my ability. With time, I stood on my own, using a chair or the broomstick to steady me.

"Well, we'll have you back to walking in no time," she said. "But for now, let me fetch Asa. I've been instructed to feed you immediately, so we'll just have you eat in the kitchens, yes?"

"Asa – doesn't he serve Matthias?"

"Oh, yes, but Matthias can spare him," Mary said.

"You think highly of him, but he is rude to me," I said with a small snort. "Perhaps it is that you see good in everyone, Mary."

She nodded as she opened the door and waved Asa in.

"Perhaps I do," she said.

Asa had me up and in his arms before I realized it, flashing a slight smile as he did so.

"Thank you, Asa," I said, looking up at the gentle giant carrying me. The sun was setting, and clouds hung low in the sky, casting a beautiful shade of pink and blue across the horizon. I marveled at it as we rounded the corner and ducked in through a small, servant access door, and wound our way through a narrow hall, following the swelling heat and aroma of cuisine.

The hall opened up to a large room filled with pots, pans, and several women glided through the kitchen, grabbing supplies and stirring their fare. Asa sat me down on a short stool and handed me the broomstick to help keep me steady.

The scent of warm food battered my nostrils. I had never eaten cooked food, and the thought was nauseating, but I felt weak and an enormous pain was growing in my stomach.

Mary donned an apron as soon as she walked through the door and joined the rest of the workers as they chopped, whisked, yelled for the young helpers to fetch this and that from the pantry. A few short minutes, and Mary handed me a bowl, filled with a thick, bubbling hot liquid and a spoon.

I eyed both, and Mary called out, "It's hot, take your time."

I would have to. Having never eaten with a spoon, I stared at it long enough for the soup in my bowl to cool, twisting the handle of it back and forth in my hand. I knew what the utensil was, but performing the action was unfamiliar.

I watched the women work, saw them pick up large, exaggerated versions of the tool I held in my hands, paid close attention as they scooped up their creations and brought it to their mouths, sipping lightly, tasting.

Following suit was difficult, unnatural, but by the time the edge of the spoon scraped the bottom of the bowl, I was functioning, although it was not pretty. Some of the food dripped down my chin, but my starvation pushed past any shame I harbored.

"You are not used to spoons, are you?"

The voice was rich and deep. *Matthias.* Several of the women heard the rumble of his voice and looked up, halting as if awaiting orders.

"Continue your work," he said, and they obliged with a harmonic "Yes, sir!" - Their stirrings and kneading and working rapidly increased by the second. They cast curious glances over to our corner as they labored.

My skin heated as I flushed with embarrassment. Lifting my hand to wipe my chin, I further smeared the dabble of food. He appeared at my side, knelt down to face me.

"Here," he said, reaching into his pocket.

A small white fabric was offered up, and I eyed it with suspicion as I reached to accept it. My movement was slow, however, and unsure, and he responded by lifting the cloth to my chin and dabbing away the mess.

"I need to speak with you, alone."

He kept his voice low, his concentration on cleaning me up. His face close to mine made me uneasy, shy. He was handsome, easily the most handsome male I'd seen onshore or in the waters, and I understood what the young washwoman had seen in him.

He was striking, *every bit of him*, and my attraction to him was undeniable and embarrassing. His touch, as I just now had found, could be so gentle, but his words and behavior toward me were so harsh.

Why did I find myself so intrigued by this man? Was I really so shallow to be drawn in by a handsome face?

Torn between the desire to slap him and kiss him, I grasped his wrist, staying his movement. It would be best if he kept his distance. Perhaps the more I would come to know him, the more I would grow to love him, but the more it would hurt to know that we could never be.

Fate was not kind, and I was blessed to have garnered its mercy once before.

"I do not need your pity, Matthias," I leaned away from him as I pushed his hand away from me.

"I pity no one, Ia," he said as he stood up. "You least of all."

47

My heart skipped a beat. Again, gentle in one moment and so abrasive the next.

"Matthias, sir," a boy stepped in to the kitchen, dark skinned and thin, resembling a younger, more gaunt Matthias. "The master is requesting you in the slave's quarters."

Matthias's jaw flexed. Everything about the way he carried himself, down to the smallest movement, told me he was holding a storm inside, and while I knew myself to be the cause of a piece of it, my instinct told me something far worse was at hand.

He nodded and walked toward the door.

He looked back over his shoulder. "We will speak later."

The door shut behind him, and a collective sigh of relief could be heard throughout the room, mine most certainly the loudest.

s i x

MY HUNGER SATIATED, ASA RETURNED me to the sleeping quarters, and I found myself for the first time since arriving, pleasantly alone. The heat still hung in the stale air, so I motioned for Asa to leave the door open as he left, hoping that the warmth would seek an exit and provide me a moment's reprieve.

Stationed at my makeshift bed, I managed to remove my clothes, leaving only a thin, sheer layer of cloth to cover me. Mary had placed the sole chair in the room next to where I would sleep, knowing I needed the help to balance.

As it would happen, I was also stationed next to the lone mirror in the room, a tall, wooden-framed marvel that we had almost stumbled into earlier.

I could've stared at my reflection for hours if Mary would have let me. It was fascinating, seeing myself for the first time in such clarity.

In the water, in my gifted form as a mermaid, I knew I was attractive, at least to the mermen.

This device, however, allowed me to see the truth of my appearance, and I found it confusing, difficult to imagine what they saw when they looked at me. I was not of any particular beauty, from what I could tell. I could easily find several sisters far more comely than I.

This human form – was it any different, aside from the legs?

I pulled the thin, white fabric against my shape as I stood, propping myself against the chair to ease the trembling muscles of my legs. I saw all my body had to show me, saw the small, round pink of my nipples pressed against the fabric, saw the triangle that formed where my legs began.

Using the palm my hand, I traced the features of my face, grazed the swell of my breasts, and followed the curve of my waist, my figure, down to my legs.

Matthias' face came out of the shadow of the doorway, and it was the green of his eyes illuminated by the moonlight, as much as his presence, that froze me in place.

His plush lips were parted, his breathing growing heavier with each moment that passed. *Those eyes* – they were changed from what I had seen earlier. There was no coldness, nor anger.

He savored me, and I let him, unsure of what I should say, and unsure of the strange stirrings this man's presence sparked within me. I opened my mouth to say something to the man who was now blatantly appraising me, but I stopped.

I liked the way he looked at me, despite his earlier abrasiveness, and as his gaze roamed my form, so did mine to his, taking in his strong, firm stature. His shoulders were wide above a broad chest and narrowed down to a lean waist.

I could see the build of his arms through his shirt, their muscles drawing tight under my attention, and *his hands*. I wanted his hands on me, everywhere his gaze touched, and I found my cheeks flushing with the thought as my yearning for his flesh built.

An eternity passed, or so it seemed, before he tightened his jaw, pursed his lips, and looked away. I released the cloth, letting its small shadow cover me.

"Here," he said, breaking the silence as he held out a long wooden stick with a curve on the end. "It is not my finest work, but I made it quickly, knowing you could use it."

"Thank you," I said, turning and reaching for his offering. The cane was heavy but sturdy. A sweet, wooden scent emanated from it and there were rough ridges where it had been carved. Placing the other end on the ground, I found it surprisingly stabilizing despite my shakiness.

"I will smooth it more tomorrow," he said, turning to leave.

"Wait," I stopped. It was ludicrous, and I regretted speaking or even indicating I had something to say. I hoped that he didn't hear me and would continue his course.

He halted, looked over his shoulder, casting furtive glances at me.

"Speak," he said.

"Do you like what you see?" I stammered out.

His eyes met mine, and he walked up to me, inches away. The heat of his breath lapped at my skin, setting me aflame. His expression hardened and softened, full of conflicting emotion. His jaw flexed, and he swallowed.

I was not sure why, exactly, perhaps it was as shallow as my appreciation for his striking appearance, but I wanted him to kiss me, to take me with the lust I had seen in his eyes.

"No," he said, through gritted teeth, and then he turned away from me and walked out of the room.

Mary gave a quick knock at the door before she stepped in, not so much to ask permission as to inform me of her entrance.

She looked down the hall, the direction Matthias had headed, her brow wrinkled in confusion, and I struggled to hide the aggravation spawned by his rejection.

s e v e n

THE NEXT TWO DAYS I spent falling, or so it seemed. My muscles were strong, and it did not take me long to stand, but walking was more difficult than I imagined. Everything about the motion was unnatural to me, a heavy chore worsened by my leg.

Asa kept a silent vigil and remained an ever-present guardian outside the door to my room to carry me in to the kitchen for my daily meal. That, too, was an experience I was unused to.

The oceans are teeming with life, and while human flesh and blood was the most nourishing (and delicious, unfortunately), other, smaller prey were always available in times of hunger. The hunger, coupled with the distress of this foreign place, robbed me of sleep, and in my restlessness, my mind circled around the memory of Lili as she plummeted.

Was she dead? Was she severely injured?

A pang of guilt, of grief, washed over me. Overwhelmed by my own situation, I had not given her and her outcome as much thought as I should. All of it still felt as though it were a dream.

When the sun rose, I pushed aside my emotions the best I could and attempted to walk, knowing that without that particular ability, my chances of returning home would lessen. The third day, with the assistance of Matthias' cane, I was able to limp along, putting one foot in front of the other. It was slow, tedious work, but with the additional support, I found myself staying upright.

Mary was pleased to see my progress when I walked into the kitchen, was quick to voice her approval.

"Tomorrow, we'll find you a place, and you can eat with us."

I smiled, but the thought at the forefront of my mind was getting back to the shore. That night, when the washing women came into our quarters, I asked them if there were positions for servants next to the water.

"That's a right odd question," Rose said. "There is nothing but fields on this end of the island, and you don't want the work of them, believe me."

The others nodded in agreement.

"But don't you say anything. Matthias will not hesitate to put you out there with them," Rose continued, not looking up for a second as she worked a needle and thread into a tear on her dress.

"We're lucky," Ann said, solemn.

"Blessed," Rose replied. "We best say a few more 'Hail Mary's lest the Master get a mind to work us more as slaves rather than servants."

"What is the difference?" I asked. Each day among these humans brought to light the reality that their world was all too similar to mine. Servants and slaves alike were Lessers.

All the women turned to me, some with wide-eyes and open mouths.

"Slaves are bought, owned. Property the *whole* of their life," Youngest Rose answered me, lying back on her bed, tucking her arms under her head. "We are contracted to work for so many years in exchange for food, shelter, and transport here. At the end, we get our freedom," she paused. "You did read your contract, didn't you?"

I shook my head. I had not the slightest clue as to what a 'contract' was, and the continual mentioning of it furthered the mystique of it. I reminded myself to ask someone, perhaps even Matthias in his moments of rare kindness.

"I don't know how to read," I said.

"Surely someone read it to you then," Ann said. "They did to me."

I shook my head again.

"What's done is done. Your contract is somewhere at the bottom of the ocean, more than likely. If you can remember who you signed it with – which company, the Master could write to them for a copy."

Shipwreck. Would it be possible to make them believe I want to search the washed up pieces for signs of my nonexistent contract? Would it be too great a falsity?

Would it be enough to get me to the water?

"I would like to go back to the shore, where I was found. See if any of my belongings might be washed ashore there."

"They would've burned it all by now, odds are," Rose replied. "You could try anyhow. We house servants are sometimes allowed an afternoon after our duties our done, once a month on a Sunday."

A month.

"And someone could take me? Asa, with the cart?"

"I'd ask Matthias. He has more freedom than the whole lot of us, being Foreman and all," Youngest Rose said.

Matthias.

The mention of his name tore me. If ever there were a reason to make my way to the sea, he would be it, and yet, I found myself wanting to linger, to watch, to *learn* him. Perhaps a month would be best, anyhow. Follow their rules, their constructs.

My slow-moving, poorly balanced form would make for a poor escape.

I would stay. I would watch, I would learn, and when the time came, I would return home.

If home was what it really was anymore.

e i g h t

"WELL, LOOK AT YOU. YOU won't be starving after all," Matthias said in a terse, sharp manner.

The sun had not quite risen when I tracked him down. He sat atop his horse, surveying the overseers as they led the workers from the quarters to the fields. My stomach had flipped as I made my way to him, my soul hoping that I would catch sight of the *kind* Matthias.

I had no such good fortune.

"I was ordered to report to you, now that I could walk, and was told that you would find a place for me to work," I said.

He scoffed, looking to the long line of toiling slaves, some already feeling the strike of leather against them. Matthias' shaded eyes watched their movements for a moment, and he blinked slightly at the sound of each lash.

Men stood nearby, some white, some African, all with whips. *Overseers.*

They watched us with interest as they mumbled their small talk. Their voices raised some, and their attention seemed divided between us and something in the direction of the manor house. I glanced in the direction the men had looked and caught sight of Lord Malcom, riding his steed at a leisurely pace toward us.

Turning my gaze back to Matthias, I saw that he, too, was now looking Lord Malcom's direction.

"I had reported for work to the house servant matron, Ms. O'Flannery," I said. "She informed me that I would not be suitable as a maid nor did the laundry and kitchens need further help."

"What are you capable of doing," he asked, turning his cold stare back to me. It felt more an insult than a question.

I stood in silence, determined not to break in front of him and bit my tongue to keep my temper.

"Stables. We lost a stable boy last week. Had his head kicked in," he said. "You can have his place, if you believe yourself able to stay out of trouble."

I gave a curt nod and turned to leave, when a loud crack burst in my ears. A stinging sensation formed diagonally on my back, first a slight tingle, then a large wave of pain. It was sharp, as though a knife had sliced across my skin, followed by a burning heat. The shock of it stole my breath, and I gasped.

Bracing myself on my cane, I breathed deeply through my nostrils, struggling to keep from crying out, pursing my lips and squeezing my jaw shut as my body shook. Much against my desire to fall, I remained standing and turned to find Matthias rolling up a bullwhip, slowly and deliberately.

"You are my charge now," he stated through gritted teeth. "Next time you fail to address me properly, I'll make your back bleed for days. Understand me?"

"Yes, sir," I coughed out, wondering if those were the words he was looking for.

"Go, and know a pretty face will not purchase you any lenience with me."

He spurred his horse as he gave me his final order, and I waited until he was long out of sight before I cratered to the ground, sobbing. The pain was inconceivable. How could anyone handle *one* of those whippings, let alone ten?

I heard Lord Malcom's voice behind me but could not make out his words.

"She will not be insubordinate next time, sir," Matthias replied.

As I gathered myself and began making my way toward the main grounds, I felt the long line of bloody beads forming across my back. The day was just starting.

ABEL WAS THE MAN IN charge of the stables. He was quiet and apparently torn between laughing and scoffing when I told him I had been instructed to work there. He threw a shovel at my feet and instructed me to clean the stalls. I had only ever been close to a horse the day they carried me in the cart. The animals terrified me, but I did my best to swallow that.

Joseph, the young boy I had recognized from the kitchen took me by the hand and had me follow along with him as he began his duties.

"You'll be helping me," he informed me with a sigh, his accent thicker any than I'd heard before. "It's hard work, it is. Last boy got killed."

He worked with haste, moving from one task to the next, and I hobbled after him as best I could, helping alongside him when there was room, fetching things for him when there was not. As we made our way to each stall, he introduced me to the creatures housed within, teaching me their names and letting them get used to my scent and voice before we entered.

Although most were gentle, a few kicked and stomped and neighed.

"Talk to them. It helps sometimes," he said, and I obliged, but my words found them more agitated.

I pursed my lips and began to hum. It was Mother's lullaby, and I calmed myself with it as I tried to adapt to my new assignment among these strong-willed animals. A few notes in, all had relaxed, softly hoofing the ground with light neighs.

Joseph looked up at me, eyes half-closed. "How did you do that?"

I shrugged as he shook himself and then pulled me by my hand around the structure to show me the rest of my duties.

It was a difficult notion, the thought of me doing all of this work by myself, but Joshua remained confident, offering praise when I managed to do something correctly and giving me gentle criticism when I complicated it. Laboring, especially shoveling was strenuous, with one leg incapable of quick movement and one arm constantly gripping the cane.

The process was slow, and I kept the shovel's handle tucked close to my body under my free arm to guide its placement. Despite his smaller stature, Joseph could easily lift twice the load that I could manage and do so in half the time. Still, he was patient, and I was all the more grateful as the day wore on.

We encountered Abel only when he was fetching a horse or returning one to its stall. In the afternoon, the horses were freed in a small pasture. The younger ones would trot and play, the others would bask in the sun. They were a beauty to behold.

"All in all, there's twenty-three horses, which is a lot for this island," Joseph told me as we carried water from the nearest well to the main trough. "Or so Matthias says. The Master likes to ride, and he breeds them to sell to the other merchants around here."

"You know a lot," I said.

"Yes, I was lucky, I was," he said, as we shoveled manure and hay. "The Master had need of someone to work the stables, and Matthias was kind to me. He gives me lessons, teaches me, although I'm not allowed to tell anyone about it."

He paused, rested a limb on the handle as his eyes narrowed.

"You won't tell anyone will you?"

I smiled. "No."

If anything, I was a little relieved that some of Matthias' good qualities were becoming more evident, but it did little to ease my anger. "Is he not allowed to teach you?"

Joseph shrugged, keeping his eyes on the pile of hay we were forming. "The master permits it of the slaves in the house, but all of us who work out here, he thinks it's dangerous."

I hobbled back into the stall we were cleaning, using the shovel as my cane until I was out of the muck, striking a careful balance as I pulled the bedding from the corner with the shovel blade for easier access.

"Joseph. Do you think he would teach me?"

A loud, purposeful sigh escaped him. "Maybe."

Getting the meeting times and location out of Joseph was like pulling an eel out of its hole. He was slippery, reluctant, and I sensed his divulgence had been more an attempt to brag a little than to open the way to an invitation.

They met as often as they could, he and Matthias, during supper, under the large tree next to the back of the horse corral. It would be a long walk for me, and with no knowledge as to whether he would accept my presence or lash me as he had done earlier, it would be a courageous undertaking, one that my stomach and back were shouting against.

61

Then again, perhaps I could make him an ally. Regardless of my current feeling toward him, if I could manage to get him to trust me, perhaps he would help me return home.

If.

He could just lash my back until there is nothing left for even asking.

The labor made my body ache; the torn strip of flesh on my back burned more with each drop of sweat, but conversation with Joseph made the time pass a little quicker. Perhaps too quick as we found ourselves rushing to finish what we'd be ordered to do for the day.

With the sun set, and the dark settling over us, I bade Joseph a good evening and began to make my way to the sleeping quarters.

A shadowy figure.

It was hard to see in the darkness, another element of humanity that I was not accustomed to. It followed alongside me for a moment, and my heart pounded in my chest as my pace quickened.

"Ia. Ia, stop!" An order, but muted. Not quite whispered.
Matthias.

I halted, struggling to see him in the darkness.

He waved, motioning for me to come near. I hesitated, the fear of his strike as fresh on my mind as the blood on my back.

"Yes, sir," I said, not bothering to keep my voice down.

"Your back," he said. I remained facing him, unsure of his command.

"Turn around so I may see it," he continued with a sigh. Using the cane to steady me, I turned, fighting the reflex to cringe.

What will he do now? Rub salt in my wound?

A light touch streaked along the abused flesh, a confused sensation, burning yet comforting.

62

"It was not my intention to strike you that hard," he said, the heat of his breath touching the back of my neck. "I cannot be forgiving in front of the others, especially Lord Malcom."

What could I say to that poor attempt at an apology? My head dropped to my chest as I sighed. Moments passed, his fingers still resting on me, before he moved, leaning closer to me.

"Lord Malcom would have you stripped and flogged until you could not move for days if you continue to forget your place."

"This was a favor to me," I said, incredulous. I snorted in disgust.

He whirled me around to face him faster than I could object, catching me as I lost my balance, steadying me by placing my hands on his chest. Solid stone underneath that thin shirt, yet I felt his heart pounding as quickly as mine.

"You are in grave danger here, Ia," he whispered, his green eyes wide and enveloping me, the sheen of them glistening in what little moonlight we had. "You are a beautiful woman, extraordinary, even with your short hair and your leg, and I fear for you."

He feared for me?

"I was able to keep you out of the house, but it was my mistake to place you in the stables."

"I do not understand," I replied.

"Stay out of sight as best you can, Ia. Keep your face down, and if you see Lord Malcom or any of the other overseers nearby, move yourself in the opposite direction before they detect you."

I nodded. He was warning me, but of what? Genuine concern was in his eyes now, not the frigid harshness that had been there this morning.

"You understand me, Ia?"

"Yes, sir," I said, breaking eye contact with him.

He nodded, convinced I had learned whatever lesson he had so violently taught me. My emotions were as raw as my back, however, and he would be a fool to believe that I felt his action justified.

I parted my lips to ask permission to leave, but I realized the servants and slaves alike operated only under commands by the person given authority over them. He would tell me when to go, and from the look on his face, he was not done with whatever he had to say.

"You may call me Matthias when we are alone." He paused, staring into my eyes. "I spoke with my mother."

I had no response, confused by what he wanted of me, what he was searching for in me. For someone so fluid in his speech, the fact he could not find the words brought even more gravity to this clandestine discussion.

"My mother. Zatia," he said, eyebrows raised, looking for recognition on my face, and even in the dark and with my poor eyesight, I saw his skin reddening. "She said when they were cleaning your wounds, with the seawater, they healed. Immediately."

It was true. I had nothing to say against it, and a lie would only anger him, so I answered him with silence, unsure of what I could possibly tell him.

"That cannot be true," he said. "That had to be an illusion, something they imagined. If they speak of this to anyone, you, *and they,* could be mistaken for witches, and I will be powerless to stop the consequences."

I let out a long exhale.

"You must tell me, truthfully, what you did that would have them believe such absurdness?"

He waited for an answer, and the longer I kept him from one, the worse it would be for me. Then again, how would he take the truth? The consequences of that might have been direr than I could imagine.

"It is true, sir," I backed up to walk away. "The salt water is healing to me and my kind."

Rage streaked his face, and I prepared for his whip. "Liar."

"I do not lie." My breath quickened. "Search my face, my eyes. Take me to the ocean, and I shall show you."

He leaned back, arms crossed, tapping a fist against his lips.

"I speak the truth. Your mother speaks the truth, and I gather she is a woman wise to many things, is she not?"

His features mellowed, and his brow smoothed and lips relaxed.

"Take me to the ocean, Matthias."

He took my hand in his and closed the distance between us.

"I do not know that I believe you, Ia, but I know you are truthful, and it confuses me," he said, turning my hand over to view my palm, his fingertips tracing the lines. "My mother follows the gods of her people. Her faith was the only thing that my father was unable to strip her of. She called you 'Mama Wata'? Does that mean anything to you?"

I shook my head.

My tribe, the whole of my clan, made their homes in the north and here, in the warmer waters. I knew of clans that lived along the shores of Africa, but had never seen them, nor did I know the languages of the humans they preyed upon.

"Who are you, Ia?"

He reached for me, and I trembled as the back of his hand stroked my cheek. He cocked his head to the side.

"Are you scared of me?"

I nodded, and he grew distant, as though he was looking far away, right through me.

"You should be." He spoke, and it was almost lost to me, soft and formed in a long exhale.

"Speak of this to no one."

"I will not say a word."

"I will come to you, once you have worked here a little longer, and will take you to my mother."

My heart leapt in my chest. She could help me, maybe even tell me if my situation was permanent. And her house was near to the water....

"And Ia," he said as he pulled me closer. His movement was powerful, as though he could crush me with his hands, and yet tenderness was in his touch as he gently lifted my face toward his. "You are exquisite and incomparable. Keep your distance from the house."

He released me, and then began to walk away.

"Matthias, wait, please," I said, swallowing my anxiety. "Will you teach me as you do Joseph?"

He stopped in his tracks, and then approached me in haste.

"Not permitted. Only house slaves may learn enough to keep them distinguished in their duties."

My brow furrowed, and hope sank a little that I could learn more about this world, maybe learn more about the puzzling man before me. Hot air bellowed out of his nostrils, and he shook his head.

"I will do this as it would please my mother, but you must not speak of it to anyone," he said, soft and low.

I nodded, and when I caught a darkening look from him, I remembered. "Yes, sir."

"Matthias, do not bring yourself trouble on my account," I continued. "If educating me is something that could endanger you, that is."

He scoffed, a soft smile on his lips.

"Do not worry for me. I will be fine. I always am."

Thoughts of Matthias lashing me, and Zatia's words came to surface, as well as Asa's back. In fact, all of the poor souls from Africa had scars. Some were more visible than others. Some were read on their weathered faces, their slouched statures, and pleading eyes.

Matthias blinked with every lash given. Was it simply from the noise, or was there empathy hiding in him? Was he flinching in disguise?

"Has? Have you?" I stopped. The question was inappropriate, and it was out of curiosity as much as of my concern for him that I started to ask. "Have you ever been...hit?"

"You mean received lashes – from a whip?"

His face darkened, lips pursed a little, and every inch of him told me before he even answered.

"More times than I care to remember and still less than my mother's people bear by the age of ten."

"I am sorry for that."

Those were the only words I could think of. It was grotesque, this place, and yet it mirrored my own. I wanted to embrace him, embrace the people made to feel of low worth, forgive him of the harm he caused me this morning. Create a place of refuge, safety, where we may exist and thrive above these divisions.

"You best get to your quarters before someone takes notice," Matthias said.

"Yes, sir," I replied, but through all this, a question still remained. I appreciated his defense, the role of guardian he had assumed over me, but *why*? Why me, and not the other enslaved ones, his mother's people, the ones brutalized day in and out in the fields?

There was something about Matthias, something troubled and yet something good, and I sensed it all in my bones.

n i n e

EXCRUCIATING. AGONIZING TO MOVE, TO BREATHE.

The soreness of my muscles made me tremble as much as the pain across my back. I cursed Matthias under my breath as I made my way to the stables. Morning had just broken, and I made out the silhouette of Joseph moving about, extinguishing the lanterns one by one as I neared. The large doors at both ends of the building were open to let the morning light in.

Abel was in the nearest pasture, working with a beautiful stallion that had been the master's most recent acquisition. The horse was a magnificent creature, his coat already glistening as he moved to Abel's commands and crack of his whip.

I knew of horses before I found myself stranded ashore, had seen them from a distance as they drew carts and carriages along the water's edge and worked about the docks alongside their masters, but never had I been allowed the close distance or time to admire the magnificence of them until I worked with Joseph.

I slowed to take the stallion in, and I found myself stopped, leaning against the fence. This horse was one of five that refused to let me near it, but tolerated Joseph quite well. I wondered if he sensed what I was underneath this fragile form.

"He is magnificent," a voice next to me said, and I looked up, startled, to see the master at my side. "Superior bloodline. If his breed had nobility, he would be King."

"Yes, sir," I said, careful to keep my head lowered as I had observed others do.

"I have not seen you in the house," he said.

"No, sir, I have been assigned to the stables."

"Indeed," he said, clicking his tongue. "I expected you to be assigned a duty in the house, but Matthias is not easily persuaded to let me have my way. Such a lovely face to be shoveling hay and manure all day."

"Thank you, sir," I replied. I swallowed and found my mouth incredibly dry.

"You shall accompany me, then," he said, offering his arm. I took it without hesitation, switching the cane to my other hand as we walked to the stables. "I purchased him from the royal estate, that one."

He nodded to the stallion.

"He is the most beautiful creature I have seen, sir," I said, and he stopped, a pleased smile stretching across his lips.

"Yes," he replied. "It pleases me to see I am not the only one on these grounds who recognizes the majesty that he is."

We neared the stables, and Matthias came from around the corner, guiding his chestnut mare.

"Ah, Matthias," the Master called, and I watched Matthias' face pale and his jaw set as he glanced from me to the man next to me. "I expected you to be in the southern fields today."

Matthias nodded. "I just came from there, sir."

His face was cool but strained, and he swallowed as he averted his sight away from me. Whatever emotion he was struggling to hide only made it more visible. Lord Malcom tilted his head to the side as he shifted his gaze between us, and then lowered the arm that had supported me.

"You best see to your duties, girl," he said, keeping his attention more on Matthias than myself.

"Yes, sir," I said, walking into the stables as fast as my body would let me.

"Where have you been?" Joseph called as he emptied a bucket of water into a trough. "You are late, you know. And today is Wednesday."

He moved quicker than I could, and I struggled to catch up to him as he made his way to the water well.

"What is special about Wednesday?"

"Every Wednesday, the master comes to inspect the horses, and sometimes, he rides out to visit the other rich people."

We were out of breath, Joseph from the frantic work and myself from keeping up with his stout, quick little legs.

"I'm sorry, Joseph, but that was who detained me."

I grabbed an empty bucket from him and attached it to the hook.

Joseph turned the crank, lowering the pail down into the well, and then paused.

"The master? He saw you?" He shook his head, muttering something under his breath.

"Yes, and talked to me as we walked to the stables."

He shook his head. "Matthias told me to hide you when the Master comes." He sighed as he jutted out his chin. "Too late now. We'll both be in trouble."

"We would surely cross paths someday, and that is a ridiculous request."

Joseph had nothing to say to my comment, instead putting himself back in our work.

Why would Matthias be worried? What harm could the master bring that Matthias hasn't already done to me in some form or fashion?

He could kill me, flog me. Then again, there are worse things than death. There are always worse things than death.

A FEW DAYS TURNED INTO two weeks, and the labor blended with the ache of my muscles until I was numb to it.

Walking became easier for me. Working in the stables developed my balance, and it became such that I only needed my cane when walking long distances, such as from the stables to the tree at the far edge of the corral for our lessons at dusk.

Joseph, as well as Abel, adhered to Matthias' wishes and sent me off on some made-up errand every Wednesday, keeping me busy until the sun reached the middle of the sky, and I could return to my required work.

The lessons that Matthias conducted in the near dark made all the effort worthwhile to me, more than I could have imagined. They fascinated me, the history, the geography, everything. Joseph would read to me, Matthias assisting only when the words were unfamiliar or difficult.

"I will teach you to read someday," Matthias told me.

He had hopes that Joseph could obtain a more esteemed position as he grew, maybe even be given an allowance to save for and eventually purchase his freedom.

"He will allow that? A slave to purchase their freedom?"

The softened side of Matthias blossomed, his guard easing as the time went on, but when I asked of the Lord Malcom or questioned slavery, he hardened back to the man I feared.

"No. If Joseph is sold, however, he may prove himself worthy to a new master, show that he is capable of becoming more than a stable boy or a farrier, though both those positions are still of merit and valued."

Joseph nodded. "Yes. I *could* be working the fields all day, every day, like all the others."

"Then I would not have such *excellent company* to work with," I said, using some of the new words I had picked up from listening to the readings. Joseph grinned at my newfound eloquence, and I thought I saw a hint of a smile at the corners of Matthias' mouth.

Sometimes Matthias was late, his duties as foreman superseding all, and on the rare occasion, he was absent entirely, with no word or explanation as to why – nor would we ever ask it of him.

Our lessons following those times found him harsh, unyielding, and impatient toward us, with not so much as a kind word.

All the other times were pleasant. The fresh air brought comfort to me, a sense of something redeeming in the middle of all this suffering. Joseph and I huddled as close as we could to the single lantern Matthias brought with him, struggling to see the pictures in Matthias' book in the fading daylight.

My first lesson was a continuation of Joseph's studies in mathematics. The numbers terrified and intrigued me, and the immediate immersion made me reconsider joining them. Joseph encouraged me, however, teaching me to the best of his ability some of what he had learned from Matthias as we worked.

Some lessons were even on manners. How one should set a table, order of seating for those with titles and nobility, all things that Matthias was confident Joseph could use to his advantage someday, even though Matthias only knew them in theory.

But as fate would have it, the small piece of contentment we'd found was all too abruptly and horrifically interrupted.

The day began as its predecessors. I awoke before dawn and made my way to the stables. No longer needing light to guide my steps across the terrain, I kept my sight fixed on the two lanterns framing the main doors. Abel, early riser that he was, had lit them sometime earlier, quite a bit earlier, or so I could tell from their weakening glow.

As I neared, I saw the doors were open, and could make out a small light from the lanterns inside. Above the neighing horses, I heard a man's voice, not Matthias nor Abel, stern and very angry.

From the way he stood, clutching the reins of a horse, I thought it to be Jasper, an overseer that was often dispatched to the town for slave purchase and trade. I had not encountered him before as Abel and Joseph were quick to send me off when they caught sight of any overseer or Lord Malcom.

I hastened my footsteps, and cringed as Jasper's rage grew, his voice rising. I could not make out all the words, just enough to know he was not pleased with something in regards to his steed, water or hay, or something of that manner, and as I entered, I expected to see Abel as the recipient of his foul-temper.

Instead, I found Joseph.

He stood in front of Jasper, blinking and shrinking as the man spat with each word. Veins popped up around Jasper's neck, the one-sided argument turning in a circle, his own words further fueling his ire. Jasper jerked, and seeing a bit and bridle hanging on one of the stall doors, he reached for it, and swung it around, building its motion until he brought it down on the poor boy.

The metal hit with a sickening thud upside Joseph's right ear, and he collapsed.

I froze, half in disbelief and half in terror, expecting the man to consider the damage done and ride off in his fury. Instead, he continued to lash at Joseph's crumpled form, striking every bit of flesh he could see, cursing loud enough that I sensed someone would hear.

My horror gave way to anger, and I no longer cared about the position it would put me in.

I would not see this boy, or any child or adult for that matter, beat to death. I threw myself on top of him, and absorbed two blows before Jasper came to some sense and realized he was no longer striking his intended target.

"What in bloody hell do *you* think you are doing, woman?"

"You are *killing* him, sir. You need to calm yourself," I hoped my advice would somehow have weight with him.

He snorted.

"I will choose when to calm myself," he yelled, the volume of his voice shaking the rafters. "Remove yourself *now*, woman, or you will join him."

Closing my eyes, I tightened myself around Joseph, trying to turn us into as small a target as I could muster. He brought his weapon down upon me, and I cried out, unable to contain the pain of it, again, and again.

"Enough!"

A voice yelled, and I knew it to be Matthias. "You will control yourself, sir!"

I cracked my eyelids open just enough to see Matthias holding Jasper's cocked arm.

"Their punishment was just, Matthias," Jasper said, his chest heaving. Matthias kept a cold expression.

"That *boy*, Jasper, is worth more than *you* when the Master chooses to sell him," Matthias said, his tone calm, collected. "You would deny him his profit because you were *slightly* inconvenienced?"

Jasper's face fell, the anger evaporating with mention of Joseph's worth, but he steeled himself again as he looked down at me.

"That," Jasper said, nodding to me, "is *nothing*. You wouldn't even want to breed her to a slave."

Matthias' jaw tensed. "We do not yet know who she may be contracted to, Jasper – or for what reason. Can you afford to purchase her contract if you render her completely useless or dead?"

Jasper jerked his arm free, dropping the bit and bridle at our feet.

"Get to your duties," Matthias said as Jasper spat on me. "I'll see she pays for her defiance."

He nodded, then mounted his horse and rode out, spurring it to run as quick as it could. Matthias watched him and waited, saying nothing until he crouched and reached for my shoulders.

"Get up. Get up now." He pulled me up, and I groaned.

"Are you injured?" he asked me as he bent to care for Joseph.

"Is he alive?" I steadied myself against an open stall door as Matthias lifted an unmoving Joseph into his arms.

"He's breathing."

Matthias carried Joseph out of the stables. I grabbed my cane and limped along, trying to keep pace.

He stopped me at the door of the quarters, out of breath and blood soaked. Matthias nodded to the mare he'd left standing outside the stables. It grazed along the path we took, making its way to Matthias. "Water her, and continue with your duties." He looked around to see who was in earshot. "I'll meet you tonight."

"Yes, sir," I nodded and guided the horse back.

My workload doubled, and I labored into the night to finish what Joseph could accomplish in an afternoon. Abel helped me where he could, but it was evident I could not replace Joseph if he were dead or injured beyond repair. I could not carry on in his footsteps.

The thought of his loss paralyzed me at the end of my day. My stomach churned along with my thoughts, and I found myself late to what would have been our lesson. Matthias was there, his face barely visible in the waning light of his lamp.

"You are late." He was chagrined and worn, stretched out on the knoll, his arms behind his head as he looked up at the sky. Small splotches of dark dotted his sleeves. I could smell it – the blood.

"I had to complete Joseph's duties as well as my own."

"Asa will assist you tomorrow."

"I don't know how to help Abel with the horses," I said, my words shaking as I sat next to him, and then laid back, my body craving the rest.

"Abel will teach you should he need the help," he said, still not bothering to look at me.

"Joseph?" I asked, fearing bad news.

"My mother is with him. She believes he will recover," Matthias said. "Although, how much remains uncertain."

Relief flooded me, and before I could restrain myself, I sobbed, covering my face with my hands as the tears flowed. Crying above the water was such an unusual sensation, so cathartic, so releasing, that I let it go, regardless of Matthias' irritation.

Warmth embraced my hand, and fingers interlaced with mine, the skin so rough and yet the touch so gentle. I uncovered my face to find Matthias on his side, propped up with an elbow, holding one of my hands, his face mirroring my pain.

"What of Jasper? What will be done with him?"

Matthias' ran a hand over his face as he sighed. "Very little. He will be docked pay for it if Joseph lives, perhaps fired or made to work off the debt if Joseph were to perish."

My jaw fell open as I shook my head. "That is all? For beating a boy nearly to death?"

Matthias nodded, slow. "He is a slave. I have no words to ease your anger."

"I'm sorry," I blubbered, embarrassed as the sobs roared up, busted out, and shook me with their force.

Grabbing my shoulder, he pulled me against him, wrapping his arms around me as I trembled. The gentle weight of his chin rested on the top of my head.

A part of me wanted to push him away, changeable and hurtful as he could be, but the larger part found peace and protection in his arms. When the tears ceased, and my raging emotions had been exhausted, I peeled my face from his shirt.

From what I could see in the low light, the tired, hurting look in his eyes, he had felt the strain of it all as well. We looked into each other's eyes, and I saw the gentle spirit and kind man that I ached to know.

The one that brought me the cane and taught me so much about his world in such a little time.

He caressed my cheek, his touch warm and inviting. Mesmerized by this maddening man embracing me, I traced his mouth with my fingertips. His chest rose and fell, and then he lowered his lips to mine, touching them, and then pressing into them. The warmth, the sensation was exquisite, and I ceased to think, my body acting instinctively as I returned his passion.

Our breath quickened as our kiss deepened, and I opened my heart to him as a flower welcoming the sun.

We stopped after our air ran out, my body aflame, every nerve in my skin tingling. Matthias sighed, long and heavy, as he nuzzled into my hair. Exhausted, I descended into slumber, into dreams of the ocean, of my sister, of Joseph, of an existence free of Callers and Masters and Guards and Foremen and Lessers.

When I awoke to the sound of the bell, I found myself tucked into my own bed. A sweet, delicate scent drifted through the air, and I turned my head to find a small, solitary blue flower next to me.

t e n

IT WAS SUNDAY.

Three weeks of hard labor passed in a blink as I awaited Joseph's return. Extensive injury prevented him from reassuming his former duties, but he helped as best he could. My body, worn and tired, drifted off to sleep in Matthias' arms at the end of many a lesson, sometimes at the start. A month had passed since my arrival, and Matthias announced he would take me to the beach for a morning's reprieve.

Matthias' moods were ever changeable in the wake of Joseph's beating. He would embrace me one day, only to lash at me with his tongue and scowl the next. I feared Sunday would come, and he would be in a cruel disposition. Much to my relief, he made good on his word.

I smoothed my skirts out with my free hand, steadying myself with the other. The sea was before me, and I took a deep breath, conflicted. The waves beckoned me, their calls permeated my bones. Closing my eyes, I opened myself to the songs they sang.

Matthias' mare nudged me with her nose, and I smiled.

"It is a fine morning, isn't it?" Matthias' voice rolled across the cool breeze.

"It is indeed."

"You seem nervous," he said as he walked around to face me, head cocked to the side. "This is what you wanted, yes?"

My nostrils flared as I inhaled the salty air, nodding. "Yes. Thank you."

"It is my pleasure," he said. "Sit with me?" He smiled and held out his hand, guiding me down to the sand with him. "Although I must be honest. This visit isn't entirely for you. The beach happens to be my favorite place on the whole island."

I grinned, and he leaned back. "I love the ocean. It's calming. I swear it sings to me sometimes."

My grin faded a little. "It calls."

"Yes, yes. Exactly." He focused on the horizon of endless water stretched out before us. "There is something very freeing about that expanse out there. When I was a boy, I used to fancy myself a pirate." He looked over at me with a devilish grin. "I would steal my father's things and bury them along the beach. I only recovered a small fraction of it, my hidden treasure." He laughed, and it was melodious, beautiful, and youthful.

"Those were easier days," he said. "Or so I remember. What about you? Something tells me you were an intelligent, stubborn child."

I laid back. "I was, but I had to be. My mother loved me unconditionally, but I was not born hers. My family treated me as one of their own, but our people? With them, it could be a challenge."

"I'm sorry to hear that. Your real mother - did she pass in childbirth?"

I shook my head. "No. I was left for death."

Matthias sat up, his face flushing red with anger. "I have no words."

The questions, the topics were all serious, but the corners of my mouth began to lift with a smile. "Thank you for your concern, but Mother cares for me and did an excellent job raising me as her own."

"Why are you smiling? This is a horrible revelation - to be left for death?"

I tried but failed to hold in my laughter. "I am sorry. It *is* horrible. It is just that I have never seen you so talkative without attempting to teach me something."

His expression softened as he nodded. "I should speak with you more, like this. I want to know everything about you."

My heart leapt into my throat as he took my hand in his. "Ia, I believe I am enamored with you."

His breath trembled a touch as he lowered his lips to mine, brushing them softly as he spoke. "I have never experienced the feelings you evoke in me."

A bell sounded in the distance, marking the time. Its ring was soft yet so intrusive.

Matthias blinked and pulled away. "We do not have much time before we must return." He looked to the water again, nodded toward it. "Would you like to go for a swim?"

Water.

The ocean.

Home.

Without realizing it, he was granting me permission to leave, to return *home*. I shuddered inside. I was so close, and yet I felt so far. Pulling my stare from the waves, I looked into those green, enrapturing eyes of his and made my decision.

"I think it's best we go back," I said, a bittersweet happiness rolling through me.

He winked, and then lifted me up onto his steed. I ran my hand through the mare's mane as Matthias mounted behind me. I relished the weight and strength of him against me. As he guided the horse up the crest of the dune, I glanced over my shoulder, contentment and uncertainty swirling as I thought on my choice.

e l e v e n

THE STABLES WERE CALM AND quiet aside from the wayward neigh of horses. The scent of fresh hay was in the air, made more pungent by the morning mist that hung around us. I found it comforting, routine and familiar.

Ensconced in my labor, a soft touch on my right shoulder startled me. It was Abel, holding the reins of a horse I did not recognize. Behind it trailed three others of the similar soft grey. A carriage past the lot of them was being repaired by two slaves and a blacksmith.

Abel motioned to the water trough, and I nodded, picking up the buckets and making my way to the well. The morning was cold, and the chill was made worse by the water I was now sloshing all over my clothing as I rushed to tend to our surprise guests.

A melodic, feminine laugh penetrated my concentration, and I looked to the path leading up to the main house, finding

Lord Malcom engaged with a youthful, brown-haired, beautifully dressed woman. An older gentleman joined them, making large strides to catch up to them, and her loud laughter again rang out, with scolds of "Oh, Father! Surely you jest."

Lord Malcom was jovial, perhaps even sober, as he spoke at length with them about his horses. They loitered near the stables as the carriage was brought back to working fashion. This father-daughter ensemble, so respected by Lord Malcom, piqued my curiosity and tempted me to eavesdrop.

"We would very much like to see young Matthias, Lord Malcom," the older gentleman said. "It has been some length since he has called on us."

I halted my work at the mention of his name and clung to the wall as I attempted to peer at them over a stall door.

"Yes, I am afraid I am to blame for that," said Lord Malcom, laughing. "He is stepping into his role quite nicely."

"Certainly a credit to the family name then," the older man said, leaning in with eyebrows raised and a smile growing wider on his face.

"Yes, he is proud to bear it," Lord Malcom replied. "Although I must admit I was reluctant to give it to him, it has been the best decision I've made, all things considered."

"Quite, quite," the older man said. "We were so sorry to hear of your loss."

Lord Malcom sighed, his shoulders slouching with the heavy weight of a dark memory. "Yes, well, thank you for your sympathy. Richard had always been an intelligent, but weak boy. His mother and I feared from his birth that he was never long for this world, but for him to reach thirty-five so readily…"

His voice trailed into nothing, and his guests stood in awkward silence.

"He had no heirs of his own, you know. Unable," Lord Malcom continued. "All our generations now rest on Matthias' shoulders, and if not his, then that detestable brother of mine."

"Matthias will marry, then?"

"Of course," Lord Malcom said. "As benefitting his station, which despite a full inheritance and my acknowledgement, is tainted by his mother's lineage."

The older man scoffed. "Perhaps in London, but certainly not here. He is a fine, capable young man."

"With a title now as well," Lord Malcom laughed.

The older man whispered something into his daughter's ear, and with that, she curtsied to them and excused herself, easing her way back to the manor.

"I know we've yet to be titled, but Mary herself is an only child," The older man spoke, almost too low for me to understand. "And the man who marries her will find a very sizable dowry awaiting him, including all our holdings here."

Lord Malcom tilted his head to the side, a soft smile on his face. "A beautiful face with a beautiful purse makes for a good match."

"Of course, all we need now is a title," the man said, eyebrows lifting again.

"Indeed," Lord Malcom said, followed by a click of his tongue. "Perhaps I may assist you in that regard."

"We would be so ever grateful, Lord Malcom." The man tipped in a shallow bow. "Well! It appears our carriage is ready to make the trip back home."

"So it appears," Lord Malcom said. "It was a pleasure to see you, Henry – and your lovely daughter. Melina Hills is always open to your family – carriage disaster or no."

"As is our humble estate is to you and yours."

"I expect Matthias to be visiting you in the near future," Lord Malcom said as they walked up the path. The carriage was resituated, the finely dressed driver already in his position as Abel assisted in harnessing the horses.

My heart stopped and my breath with it. Under the small talk and light sentences, they were forming a *marriage* contract. Though I was new to their world, I had heard of such arrangements between powerful families seeking to ensure a beneficial match for their children.

Matthias would be mated to an influential, rich family - not the likes of a limping stable hand.

Work slowed as I dwelled on it, much to my shame. The strong feelings I had for him, the passionate kisses we shared, had blinded me.

Laboring into the evening, I heard the gallop of hooves in the distance and looked up. From the build of his silhouette, I knew that it was Matthias. A light trailed down the path after him.

"Matthias!" Lord Malcom was now alone, striding toward him, calling out until he reached the doors of the stable, his rigid frame watching Matthias as he neared.

"Good evening, sir." Matthias dismounted next to him.

"You missed a fine opportunity earlier." Lord Malcom smiled. "Our neighbors to the north paid us a visit."

I continued my work, straining to hear their words as I shoveled fresh bedding in a stall on the opposite end of them.

"I have no interest in marriage to his daughter, sir, and to fan that flame would be only to her detriment," Matthias said, his volume rising above the noise of the horses.

"Wake up, boy. You will marry who I say you shall marry," Lord Malcom said. "Do you know how fortunate you are that I chose to give you my name? *Mine*? You could be out there a slave, and yet I chose to claim you as my son."

I peeked around the door stall I was standing in and watched Lord Malcom's face flush.

"I have done nothing but *heed* you since I was born, much to my disgust," Matthias said. "I have whipped, *beaten*, people who did nothing but displease you because you ordered it. I have given away my soul to be your son, and I will not yield the last bit of goodness I have in me because you desire me to marry a spoiled brat with a swollen purse."

"It's that girl, isn't it? The crippled one from the shipwreck," Lord Malcom said. "The one you coddle and pity. Do not think for a moment that I do not know you spend every free moment you have near her."

Matthias' hands tightened into fists.

"Bend her over a barrel and be done with her," Lord Malcom continued. "She is a *servant*, Matthias. She is property, *my property*, and once you have your way with her, you will not associate with her further, do you understand me?"

"I will do no such thing," Matthias said.

"You will not defy me," Lord Malcom said. "You will deeply regret it if you do, as would your mother and aunt and that *girl*."

Matthias shook his head, his shoulders slumped.

Lord Malcom scoffed. "You are welcome to join your mother's family in the fields if you wish. I will have her and your aunt join you. It is your decision."

His voice grew lower, until I could hear no more, only the clicking of hooves as Matthias neared, guiding his horse to her stall.

I stepped out, and Matthias sighed as he saw me.

"Are you well?"

He shrugged, looking away from me.

"He's sending me to town to trade." Matthias ran a brush down the back of his horse. "It is deplorable. Nothing but terrified people auctioned off as though they were livestock."

He paused. "I will be gone a day, perhaps two. He is attempting to force me to marry and accept his inheritance under threat of enslaving and possibly killing my mother."

I stood next to him, combing the mane of the mare who nibbled at me as I moved.

"What will you do?"

"*We*, Ia. You and I and my close family, will leave, someway, somehow," Matthias said. "I cannot stomach the man he would have me be. It was difficult enough when he made me Foreman." He rested a hand on top of mine.

We moved in silence, side-by-side.

"I know the monster that sired me, and he will do *something* to you while I am away, I am sure of it," Matthias said. "I may be gone for more than a day, and I cannot take you with me. Go to my mother's home, claim illness, injury, anything. It will buy you time until I return."

I nodded.

"While I am away, I will find the next ship to leave this godforsaken place and purchase our passage on it," Matthias continued. "Ia, do not go back to your room tonight. Seek my mother immediately. Do you understand?"

"The few belongings I have - my clothes - are there."

"It is not worth the risk," Matthias said. "Feed and water my horse while I gather what I can."

I halted. "You are leaving *tonight*?"

"Lord Malcom insists we be there at first light." He repositioned the saddle, watching as the glow from torches appeared in the dark, tracing a route toward the sleeping quarters of the field slaves. "It appears he has already sent some of the overseers to help me on my way."

He sat down the brush, turning to me, and before I could react, he wrapped me in his arms. My heart pounded as my chest touched his, as his lips grazed mine, and then he kissed me. I savored his scent, his taste, and the safety I felt in his arms.

"Come back soon," I said. "Please."

"I will, and I *will* seize the opportunity to set our plans in motion."

He mounted, keeping saddened eyes locked on me as he rode off, steering his horse to a line of wary chain-clad slaves ambling down the road to the cracks of their overseers' whips.

t w e l v e

"IA, YOUR PRESENCE HAS BEEN requested for dinner."

The silver-haired butler from the main house stood straight-backed and nose titled up, wrinkled from the smell of the dung I had been shoveling.

I halted as shiver worked its way up my spine. Matthias had told me to leave, to go to his Mother's, and I was on my way, but I could not very well leave tools and buckets and everything laying out, abandoned. Not only would it raise suspicion, it would cause trouble for all who worked the stables.

"I am sorry, sir, but I am unwell. I am on my way to the home of the healer, with permission of the Foreman, of course," I said, determined to walk past him and direct myself to Zatia.

His outstretched arm halted me, stopping but inches from my chest.

"You do realize that this is an order from Lord Malcom?"

"Would he wish illness upon himself?"

The man shrugged. "Lord Malcom will decide that for himself. I will inform him, but in the meantime, you shall follow me."

"No," I replied.

His jaw fell open. "Please, for your sake as much as my own. Lord Malcom is not a man to cross."

The look in his eyes was a pleading one, and as I gazed around him to avoid it, I noticed movement between us and the manor. A couple of the overseers that had been left behind were standing on the path, watching our interaction.

"If you do not come with me willingly, then they will drag you in," the man said, hiding the words in his breath, his lips hardly moving. "Smile, nod, and walk with me."

I complied, painting a smile on my face as he escorted me past the men who fell in line behind us until we reached the servant's entrance. I let the expression fall, my eyes narrowing as the man lead me down a hall, where he opened a door. The room was large, simple compared to the other furnishings of the house but elaborate compared to my small bed and shared room.

Ms. O'Flannery waited for me there, looking down her nose at me through half-opened eyes, and standing next to an open wardrobe with an array of dresses hanging therein.

"Select one, and I shall assist you in dressing," she held her hands clasped in the front of her dress. "Once you have bathed, of course."

"Of course," I said, my thoughts a flurry. If Lord Malcom had wanted me, it was within his power, disturbingly so, to take me. I had nowhere to flee, no help in doing so. He'd simply have to open the door to the room I slept in, stumbled his way through, and force himself upon me as he and the overseers were rumored to do with the field slaves.

I could fight him, but there would be little I could do and no one to come to my rescue.

Why all this trouble?

Maybe he intends to sell me, along with a forged contract, and means to introduce me to potential buyers tonight. He did complement me more than once on my beauty.

Or, perhaps, he means to assign me to house duties to keep Matthias' interaction with me limited.

That seemed the lesser of the evils eating at my thoughts, and it made sense, at least to me, that Lord Malcom would expect any servant assisting with dinner to be dressed appropriately.

"Will you be training me?"

"I beg your pardon?" Mrs. O'Flannery half-laughed.

"To serve. Proper serving," I said.

She snorted. "You? Serve? Hardly appropriate," she drew out 'hardly' as she looked down at my cane. "You will be dining *with* Lord Malcom."

I choked on my own breath. "Excuse me?"

"I trust you know how to bathe, yes?" Her voice had the same, flat tone that she'd kept in our previous encounters. My presence, especially in the house, offended her for reasons beyond my understanding. A few loud claps of her hand, and several of the housemaids appeared carrying buckets of water that they poured into a large wooden tub.

I bit my tongue.

"I shall leave Bess to attend to you. She will fetch me when you are ready to be dressed."

And so she left us, two fragile, unsure young women.

"I really do not need help, Bess. Please feel free to rest," I said. "My balance is much better than it used to be, and I only need help stepping in and out."

She nodded, and came to lend me a shoulder.

The water was hot. I had never felt anything so exquisite. Warm waters were always my favorite, but hot? I had never encountered that. I wiggled my toes, letting my muscles have a moment of relief.

"Bess," I said, on the verge of a question as I lifted a pitcher to pour the warmth over my head.

"Oh, stop!"

She jumped up off the edge of the bed and walked toward me with an outreached hand. "You must not do that. We have oil and powder to clean your hair with, and we do not have time to dry it."

Relief covered her as I sat the pitcher outside the tub.

"I'm sorry. I am lost," I said.

She nodded with sympathy.

"It is not normal for Lord Malcom to eat with a servant, is it."

Bess looked down at her feet for a time, took a breath, and looked up at me. "It is from time to time. If he finds the servant…pleasing."

"Pleasing," I repeated.

Her choice of words deepened my fears, made my stomach swim with nausea. I was not blind to the way Lord Malcom examined me when he first saw me, and again when he visited the stables.

"Yes. Pleasing. Attractive," she replied, swallowing down half of her words as though it pained her to speak them.

My chest tightened. Everything about this felt wrong from the moment his butler startled me. Matthias had warned me, warned me well, and there I was, in a room made for a clandestine affair.

"The man in the manor does not show kindness freely. Everything has a price, and you would do well to remember that," Matthias had said to Joseph and me.

It was true. Something was to be expected of me, though what, I had only a small idea. One that brought a flush to my face and a tremble to my limbs.

Lord Malcom was no better than Ro. I was his Lesser, one prettied up and made to be something pleasing to him.

He was thorough, too, sending Matthias away. Matthias was not here to save me, and had he been, he would be as helpless as the rest of us. It would be up to me to dissuade him in any way I could. Fleeing was no longer an option, at least not until Matthias returned.

My hands were shaking as Ms. O'Flannery slid the dress over me. The weight of it dropped, and I lost my balance, taken aback by it, catching myself on the post of the bed. Even while she styled my crudely shortened hair with Bess, she breathed not a word to me.

She worked as quickly as she could, jerking the strands of my hair here and there with considerable, purposeful force.

"Has Matthias returned?" I asked, voice cracking.

"No," she said.

My mind swarmed with ideas and terrors and hopes the rest of my physical preparation, until Ms. O'Flannery announced the finality of it, my transformation complete. I walked to the mirror, amazed by the person I saw in its sheen. I looked nothing like myself.

The dress overwhelmed me in all directions until it reached my waist, where Ms. O'Flannery strained and groaned to tighten the laces. The tops of my breasts, full and firm, peeked out of the square neckline. They rose and fell with my breath.

Mrs. O'Flannery thrust my cane at me and opened the door. The butler stood vigil in the hall until I was deemed adequate for their employer, and then motioned for me to accompany him.

The halls were narrow, more so than I remembered, and swallowed me as the skirts of my dress touched both sides. I held them to me as best I could and struggled to keep up with the quick-footed man in front of me. Just as I was preparing to tap my cane to tell him to stop or slow down, we came to the end, and he pushed a door open. The light from the room we were entering was soft and tender.

It was the main foyer, what I had seen a glimpse of the day I arrived, and I realized I had changed very little since then. Still afraid, still naïve, and still under someone else's control.

When would my life be my own?

Lord Malcom stood as I entered the dining room, waited for me to sit as a footman pulled out a chair for me.

"Good evening, Ia," he said, his smile relaxed, and his eyes cold.

My pasted on smile did me well. I adhered to the subjects Matthias taught Joseph and myself, and he made his compliments on his son's desire to better the world and educate the slaves.

"You could do worse, you know," he commented, swirling brandy around in his glass. I studied him, everything about him, and at times I caught a glimpse of his son in him. At other times, I saw the predator that he was.

"What do you mean, Sir?" I asked through gritted teeth, hoping the alcohol sitting before me would render this night nothing more than a horrible dream.

"I do not extend such offers lightly, nor do I extend them often," he said, his words floating as though this was still light conversation.

"I usually enjoy the pleasures of the more rotund, comely women you see in the fields, but then again, I have always had a fascination for the unusual. Such as yourself." He nodded, raising his glass to me.

I raised my glass in kind, and questions swirled around me. I could not keep them from my face.

What does he plan to do to me?

"You seem lost, Ia," he said.

I struggled to reply, stammering over my words at first.

"I wish to ask you something, sir, if I may." My throat was parched, and I reached for a glass of water.

"You may speak freely for now."

Folding my hands in my lap, I raised my eyes to his.

"Why did you invite me to dine with you?"

He laughed. "It pleases me."

I nodded, but my mind searched for the words to ask him his intentions.

"Let us speak as friends would, yes?" he said, half-asking for permission that was not mine to deny. "You are indeed receiving an honor. Your dresses, your room, your new station."

Ah. There it is.

The blatant truth. This *arrangement* was not to be for tonight alone. It would be until he tired of me, and would certainly not end until he felt Matthias would bend to his will again.

"You should know that I do value you," he said, attempting to balm the wound opening at my core. "There have been only two women to have been blessed enough to have my favor bestowed on them. The last was Matthias' mother, then again, she was a unique beauty - such as yourself."

He took a sip of his brandy, and stared off at one of the many paintings on the wall of his homeland.

"She bore me a son, Matthias. Illegitimate, of course, but a son that could rule over this place in my stead. My gift to her was her freedom, as well as that of her sister, but I digress."

Sitting down his glass, he stood and walked to me.

"He has done well with his discreet education," he said, his voice growing heavier with each breath. "I daresay you may someday pass as a lady."

My stomach fell to the floor, my resolve to find a way out of this mess sinking with it.

"You want me because of Matthias."

"Yes. Your beauty helps, however. I would have had my way with you and been done, but I *see* the way he looks at you," he said. "And his opinion may change when you are used up and nothing is left."

I shuddered as he walked behind my chair, trailing his hand along my shoulders.

"He will learn that to pine for a slave is foolish, and he will marry according to the name I've blessed him with. He should have simply eased his loins and gotten you out of his system."

"If I refuse?" The words escaped my lips, a desperate thought.

He caressed a wayward strand of my hair, and he breathed in my scent.

"I would tie you, your limbs spread apart, then rip the rags off your back, and let any and every male with an itch in their loins fuck you. When the whole of them are through, I would have Matthias himself lash your back until there is no flesh left," he whispered.

My breath caught in my throat, and my chest clenched. He could do it. He had the means, and I had the inability to escape.

"I would string up that slave stable boy you and Matthias are so fond of, and I would set him aflame for good measure. Matthias *knows* how I dislike one taking the education I paid for and throwing it away to the likes of slaves. Present company included."

He held out his arm, and I knew it was time.

I downed the rest of brandy in front of me, and then stood, taking his arm. We navigated the passages without a word until we reached the room I had been made ready in. He pushed the door open, and for the first time, I noticed the enormous bed.

Four pillars formed the corners, stretching up to the ceiling, supporting a large, scarlet canopy draped in sheer panels. Every bit of the wood was carved. At the head of the bed was a beautiful mermaid carved in intricate detail. Her arms were stretched toward the sky, and the water splashed around her lower body as she surfaced, forming the edge that framed her. She was extraordinary, and the sight of her comforted me as much as it made me long for home.

I thought of Matthias as I felt the tug of Lord Malcom's fingers on the laces of my dress. Would he look on me with shame? Would he turn away?

Lord Malcom was agile, and in a few moments, he had undone me, the dress left amid the dirt on the floor. Only the thin undergarment was left to shield my nakedness from him. He reached for it, but I stopped him by sliding my shoulders out, letting it fall.

He smiled, devouring me as he removed his topcoat and loosened his breeches, opening the falls to reveal his erect flesh. Aside from his coat, he removed no other clothing. Instead, he pressed against me, backing me to edge of the bed, and then pushed me onto it, crawling over me. The smoothness of the fabric along with his erection sent my skin crawling.

The pain of it – all of it – was unbearable. His mouth was far from gentle. He nipped at my neck, slobbering as he rammed into me again and again. I closed my eyes, trying to keep my mind on every fond memory I could conjure as his body labored over me, pawing at my breasts, growing rougher by the second. Tears formed in the corners of my eyes, and I struggled to breathe under him and the heat he was creating.

As I began to sob, I found Mother's lullaby on my lips, the one she would sing to me when terrors of the night would fill my dreams. At first, I mouthed the words as I clenched the sheets underneath me in my fists, combating the hurt surging in my loins. I found myself humming it as I did to the horses, and in an instant, all movement stopped.

He remained in me, his swollen flesh, but he moved not, just held himself suspended above me. Cracking open my eyelids, I found him frozen, brow furrowed, eyes wide and vacant.

I turned my face, and he opened his mouth to speak, but nothing came out. He pulled free from me, his once-swollen phallus now falling, and without so much as a word, he tucked himself back into his pants, and left the room.

I leapt from the bed and crawled to the nearest corner, long beyond the ability to cry, and there I slept, among dust and filth. My dreams were of little comfort. All I could see was Matthias looking down on me, filled with hurt and disgust. Not even offering up an insult, he looked at me, his father's *property*, and walked away.

This was what it felt like to be a Lesser.

The next morning Bess pulled me from the corner and guided me to the tub to bathe. Rose was with her, and operated in silence. I feared their thoughts, their opinions of me, but when I dared to meet their gaze, all I saw was pain and sympathy. After Bess removed the blood-stained sheets from the bed, Rose laid a gentle hand on my shoulder as I retreated to my corner.

"We best get you dressed," she said. "Fresh air would do you good."

I shook my head, terrified I would leave the room, and I would see Matthias, and he would know.

"You are brave, girl," Rose continued. "But you should learn when to take help. I'll go with you. Bess saw to it that I would help you for today."

"Will he come again," I asked. "Tonight?"

Rose sighed. "More likely than not. He's not as young as he once was."

"He gave me no choice, Rose." I said, confident she wouldn't believe me, but knowing that the words still needed to be said.

"We know, child," Rose said, running a comb through my wet hair. "More of us know than you could imagine. At least it was just the master and not a line of the overseers."

She left it at that, and I cared not to speak as I stepped into the bath she had prepared for me and scrubbed my skin raw.

thirteen

IT WAS A SOLID TWO weeks before Matthias darkened the doorway. Bess told me that Lord Malcom dispatched new orders for him every morning and evening, even sending more slaves to be sold and commanding him to wait on a ship from a nearby island.

I was a prisoner in the room, the entrance unlocked only to allow Bess to attend to me for the first few days. Confident thereafter that I would not flee, Lord Malcom began to leave my chamber unlocked, but he stationed a guard, usually a servant, nearby. I saw them each time the door was opened, except for when Lord Malcom would visit. I stopped counting after the fifth time.

Now, I could feel Matthias' presence behind me. My skin tingled, and the hair on the back of my neck rose up. I glanced over my shoulder, caught a glimpse of him from the corner of my eye. His weight shifted from one leg to the other, and his right hand gripped the doorframe.

Indecisive. Does he stay, or does he go?

The smell of him was intoxicating. It hurt. Hurt to be so confused by this conflicted man. Would he help me or would he leave me, turn his back as he had on all those in the fields?

I waited for words, but none were spoken. This room, so large and grossly decadent, felt so small. I stood but kept my back to him, choosing instead to cast glances over my shoulder.

"Lord Malcom has forbidden me to see you," he said. "He is visiting the estate to the north in attempt to arrange my marriage."

"Are you to leave me to him, then?"

I kept my gaze averted, not wishing him to see the shame and fear in my eyes.

He bit his lip and looked at the hem of my dress scraping the floor.

"Is that what you wish?"

His words were muffled, almost mumbled.

"No," I replied, softly.

He scoffed as he stared at me. "It suits you."

"Being a whore," I spat at him, my mouth filled with venom as I turned to face him.

"The dress."

"Where were you?" I said. "You were less than a day's ride from here."

He shook his head. "I was kept in town. I suspected it was a rouse, but I believed you to be safe with my mother hiding you. I did not realize he had you, Ia, and I had no one around me that I trust."

My ire built higher with my shame, and I shook my head.

"No?" Matthias asked, eyebrows raised.

"I do not believe you," I said. My gaze met his. "I believe you were too weak to fight for me just as you are too weak to stand up for those trapped in the fields."

His mouth fell open as his brow furrowed.

"You think me weak," he said, his face flushing red.

"*Yes*. And so cruel sometimes I think you hate me. So kind sometimes I think you might love me," I squeezed my hands to each other to keep myself from breaking down.

"Cruel? *I'm* cruel?" His posture straightened, and his hands tensed at his sides.

It was the first time he had raised his voice to me.

"Do you not see that I'd rather you feel the bite of a whip any day than hang from a noose? Do you not realize how it pains me to see people – *my own kin*, even - used like animals?! Do you not see I have to do it to keep them – *and you*- alive?"

I was frozen. All that conflict, that harshness. He was caught in the middle. Only, his body was used to dole out the master's punishment while mine was now assigned to satisfy his pleasure.

"You must speak calmly or someone will hear you."

"He is not here, and not a one of those bastards out there would dare say anything, let alone stand against me." Matthias' jaw twitched, his eyes following my curves.

"Tell me, truthfully." His voice was calm and unwavering. "Are you his whore now? Did he buy you with dresses and jewels?"

My limbs felt heavy, numb, along with my nerves. I was past the point of feeling hurt.

"You forget your place, sir. We are nothing but property, aren't we?"

I walked toward him, began to push past him.

"You are right, but goddamn it, you answer me," he said, whipping around and slamming the door with all his might.

The force of it shook the whole wall, and I thought it might crack.

"No. I will never be his," I said, my voice just above a whisper, my body and spirit worn out. "There are no dresses or jewels or freedom or anything in this world that could buy me."

His shoulders slumped as he breathed out, his body appearing as defeated as I felt, but he looked into my eyes with something different entirely – relief.

"I've been locked in here, and even if I weren't, I don't think I could've escaped without you," I said, my voice beginning to quiver. I paused.

"I wish I were new again, Matthias."

The words poured out of me. Everything I had wanted to say was bubbling to the surface.

"I wish it were *your* hands that I first felt on my body, *your* lips on my skin."

Before I could say more, he wrapped his arms around me, squeezing me close.

"I wish I could take it all back. I do. I would give anything to," I said, and his grip tightened around me, cocooning me with the strength in his arms. "Why didn't you take me for your own? Why?"

"I should have," he replied, and the warmth of his breath grazed my ear. "I should have escaped with you that night you cried in my arms."

I looked up at him, surprised to find a soft smile forming on his lips.

"Ask me." He reached to the back of my dress. His expression was serious. My fingers brushed against the back of his hands as he worked to loosen my laces, sending my heart pounding against my chest.

"Ask you what?" I pulled my arms free of the sleeves, and the fabric tumbled to the floor, leaving my body covered only by a thin, sheer shift. He grasped it, clenched it against my back, pulling it tight to my curves until each one could be seen, until the pink of my nipples showed through.

"The question you asked me that night while you stood in front of the mirror. Ask it again," he said, his tongue wetting his bottom lip.

"Do you like what you see?" I breathed out, my body tingling with the anticipation of his touch.

"Every bit," he said, his voice dripping with the desire that ruled his expression and quickened his breath. "You do not perceive how breathtaking you are, Ia, do you?"

"Perhaps you could help me understand," I said, reaching up, lightly running the tips of my quivering fingers along his bottom lip.

His nostrils flared with a slow, deep breath, and then he lowered his face to mine, pressing his lips, soft and moist, against mine, grazing his tongue across my lips with each deepening kiss.

Devouring me, he dug his fingers into the material at my back, and then plunged his tongue into my mouth, finding me ripe and willing.

My whole being trembled as he explored me with his strong, masculine hands. He slid them down my waist, and then he moved his palms around to my back and down to my bottom, where he lingered lightly above before filling his hands with my rounded flesh as he covered the rise of my breasts with kisses and moans.

Intoxicated by him, I reached for the bottom of my shift and peeled it over my head, almost losing my balance. He caught me in his arms, sweeping my legs out from under me, and he carried me to the bed. Quick yet careful was his movement as he lowered me upon the cushions.

With a knee placed on the edge of the bed to steady himself, he took off his shirt, maneuvering with a slower pace as he studied every inch of me. My skin flushed, and I felt the heat flood my body beneath his appraisal.

He reached for my foot, and it jolted me. Instinctively, I pulled away, conscious of my misshapen limb. Smiling, he lifted it and placed a gentle, soothing kiss. He did the same for the other, too, his hands caressing my flesh as he moved from my ankle to my knee. My heart fluttered as I watched him go farther up the length of my leg, my breath catching as his lips grazed my inner thigh. I clenched the bed beneath me, unsure of what to do, moving fast into uncharted territory, and reeling from the unfamiliar, exciting stirrings.

Releasing my leg, he took my hand and pressed his lips to it, watching my reaction. The light in his eyes melted me. I smiled, and he placed my hand on top of his head. I weaved my fingers through his locks, delighting in the short waves that I had longed to run my hands through since I had first met him. Holding my touch there, he lowered himself back to the smooth skin of my inner thigh.

My face grew hot as he kissed up to the bend where my leg met my body, so *close* to the most intimate part of me. I so longed for his hands, even his lips, to touch me there. He paused, studying my face as he raised an eyebrow and ran his fingertips up the inside of my other leg. I shivered, unable to breathe as his fingers hovered above my core.

Slowly, he lowered his hand, skimming my flesh. A small, quick moan escaped me, and he grinned as he his pressed his fingers against me and rubbed, moving up until they reached the spot they had been searching for.

My mouth fell open, and my breath turned shallow and quick as lust and hunger overcame me, yearning for him to slide into me, to take me as I so desperately needed.... as we both so desperately deserved. I closed my eyes, consumed by the vibrations his gifted touch was shooting through me, when I felt something soft and wet take the place of his agile fingers. His mouth, his tongue worked against me, sucking and tormenting me.

A groan ripped from my throat, and I tightened my hold on his hair, clenching it as my hips lifted, grinding. His hands searched until they found the part of me that yearned for him most as I shuddered with mounting pleasure. Ever so carefully, he slid them in and out, making me aware of the abundant wetness he had provoked.

I cried out, laboring to breathe, and my chest heaved, as he worked faster and faster, pulsing in and out, consuming me voraciously with his mouth. The world around me slowed, and the depths of me lighted in flame as my mind silenced, yielding to the waves of pleasure that rolled through me, my form clenching and relaxing all at once. All control was gone, and I floated in a delirious paradise.

Sensing my wash of euphoria, he relented, and his gaze found mine. His eyes were less mischievous, less playful now. His countenance was darker, more serious. He was straining for control. He licked his bottom lip, tasting me.

"I want you, Ia," he said.

"I am yours, Matthias," I replied, my voice hoarse.

I sat upright and leaned into him, eager. I reached out, my hands searching and seeking, and was surprised when I found his hardness arousing. His desire for me rekindled the carnal fire I thought had exploded just a moment before.

My appetite to please him as he had done so readily to me grew ravenous as I reached for the top of his pants. With shaking fingers, I released the buttons until his cock, bulging beneath the fabric, pushed free.

The sight of him, erect and eager, urged me on. I traced a finger along his flesh, and his breath caught in his throat as I closed my hand around him, sliding up and down his length.

He dropped his head back, and I leaned forward, dragging my tongue across his skin until I reached the tip.

A moan escaped him as I wrapped my lips around him and slid down, taking him fully into my mouth. He balled up his hands in my hair as he pressed into me. I caressed his thighs, and I felt the tension in him I explored his body. He was holding back.

Building momentum, I slid my tongue around him, taking him in as deep as I could bear. A low, guttural growl rumbled out of him, and he pulled himself free of me.

Confused, I began to ask him what I had done wrong, but his mouth silenced mine. He nipped voraciously at my lips, and slipped his tongue between them as his hands eased down to my bottom and to my thighs.

I could taste, smell the remnants of me on him. He laid me back on the bed and lowered himself over me, pressing his cock against my wetness. Steadying himself with an extended arm, the tip of him pushed in, and I arched my back, caught in limbo between the pain and pleasure of his girth.

"I, I can't," he said, breathless. "I can't hold back anymore. I'm sorry."

With my heartbeat drumming in my chest, I opened my legs wider, my palms roamed the length of his abdomen, feeling the taut ridges. He plunged in, the whole of him, and a cry of pleasure escaped me. My hips lifted to meet his and moved with him as his pace quickened.

Mad with desire, I bit the lobe of his ear, extracting unintelligible mutterings from him. Without warning, he leaned back – the length of him inside me – and lifted my feet, resting them against his shoulders. He reached for me, and his fingers found the spot that had awakened such fervor and began rubbing quickly as he tilted into me, the weight of him pushing my legs toward my body, tightening me around his shaft.

Waves of exhilaration rolled over me again, pulling me out to a sea of ecstasy, and I soared to heights I hadn't known existed. I cried out as he thrust into me, his fingers keeping to their rhythm as I writhed, the rapturous currents dragging me under once more. He groaned and trembled as his wetness spilled inside me, and he quivered with what I knew to be the same pleasurable release I was experiencing.

Collapsing onto me, he buried his face into my neck as he fought for breath. I cradled him next to me and kissed him as we lay entwined, satisfied and euphoric.

There we stayed, enveloped in our own paradise for a while.

SLEEP WAS LIGHT, AND WHAT felt to be a short time had passed when a knock jolted me. Matthias launched out of the bed without a word or care for clothing. Opening the door, he found Asa there, motioning, his eyes wide and stressed.

"Hurry, Ia, he is returning earlier than expected," Matthias said, grabbing clothes and pulling them on as quick as he could, helping me to do the same. "We have little time. He's coming from the estate to the immediate north of us."

After pulling me through the halls, he soon gave up and swept me up in his arms, using a kick to open the door where Asa waited with a wagon. Matthias laid me gently in the back, and then jumped up onto the bench, grabbed the reins, and spurred the horse on. Two bags sat next to me, too full to be tied shut. They were filled with items that Matthias would use to barter for our passage: fabric, jewelry, a gilded candlestick.

"Matthias – your mother," I called out, half-whispering.

"She is to meet us at the docks with my aunt and niece," he said.

My heart and spirit lifted as we neared the town. I could make out the masts of the giants that sailed the seas, and an uneasy tremble flowed down my body as I saw my sister, Lili, disappear motionless into the darkness of the deep.

We found a tavern, rat-ridden and sailor-inhabited near the ship that Matthias had a mind to sail on. Zatia met us after securing Jiba and Nattie in a room upstairs, guiding us to where we would hide until night fell. Matthias bribed the captain to leave a day early and under the cover of night, using most of the items and gold he had carried in the bags. He even had the foresight to forge a Certificate of Freedom for Asa using Lord Malcom's seal.

The stench of alcohol and urine battered my senses. While the tavern keeper, with his greasy beard and black-toothed grin, eased my anxiety with his friendly demeanor, his buxom red-haired daughter ogled me with pouted lips and an evil eye. She swaggered to the corner that Matthias had stationed us and smiled as she leaned over to fill his cup with ale, her breasts nearly spilling out of the top of her ratted bodice. She winked to him as she stood up, and then cast glances his way over her shoulder as she attended other tables.

Under the brim of his hat, Matthias watched me stiffen, and heat rose to the surface of my skin at the gall of her. He waved her away, placed coinage on the table, and took me by the hand, leading me up the rickety stairwell toward the chambers.

"We need to leave," I whispered. "Now."

He shook his head, pressed a finger to his lips, and he tapped against a wall. Wood planks pulled back to reveal a hidden door, and behind it stood Zatia, Jiba, and little Nattie. I gave each a quick embrace as Asa sealed the entrance behind us.

"We must wait for nightfall," Matthias said in hushed tones.

"I do not like the look of that woman downstairs," I said. "I do not trust her."

"Her father is a good man, and I have paid them both adequately to conceal us here for the time being," Matthias said, placing his hands on my shoulders. "Try to leave your worries with me. Think instead of the life we will have together."

He placed a kiss on my forehead and pulled me tight against him. "God, you free me."

A soft knock interrupted us, and Matthias pushed himself out of our embrace as the tavern keeper poked his head in through the door, motioning for Matthias to follow. "I must attend to further arrangements. I shall be back soon."

I nodded, releasing his hand as he backed into the hallway.

"You have saved him, you know." Zatia moved over to allow me to sit next to her. "He has a *will* again, thanks to you."

When night fell, we left our sanctuary, making our way to the ship that would carry all of us to our freedom. The sky was black, moonless, with only a smattering of stars to guide us. Asa took a torch from the tavern keeper who wished us well as we crept out the back of his establishment.

Excitement built and spread throughout our small group, and our pace quickened until I found myself struggling to keep up. Matthias halted, swept me up in his arms, and carried me as we wound through the filthy back passages.

We reached the docks, which were empty, save for our ship on the end. The crew bustled about, finishing the final load of cargo.

A collective sigh of relief was breathed among us, and even in the weak light of the torch, we made out joy in each other's expressions. We were close, almost able to make out faces of the crew when men stepped out of the shadow between us and our freedom.

The overseers.

Lord Malcom lit a torch, holding it out to view us.

"Seize them," he ordered, and before Matthias could sit me down to fight them, Jasper struck him upside his head with a short, heavy wooden stick. Matthias lost his balance, and we both fell to the ground.

My head struck the stone path, and then the world slipped into nothingness.

f o u r t e e n

HE HAD BEEN TRUE TO his word, at least when it came to me. My body was broken, my spirit more so, and as I hung from the wooden poles he erected for me, my wounds pouring out my life, all I could think about was Matthias.

What would become of him?

Although my ears rang, muffling most of the sounds, I could hear wails. Asa dangled by a rope in a large tree to my left, lifeless. I shivered as much from the breeze cooling the blood on my skin as from the tears I wept when I watched them string him up.

I thought to plea, beg, scream, anything to spare him, this gentle giant and beautiful soul that showed me – showed everyone - such kindness. No words came, barred by the reality that there was nothing I could say to sway this vindictive man. I could only close my eyes and grieve, sometimes straying into vindictive thoughts myself.

There was no guarantee I'd be spared Asa's fate. No promise that I'd live to make it to the water, and little hope that I could lure that evil shell of a man there to tear him limb from limb.

Rose, the only brave one from the house servants who bore witness to my torture, brought me water when she felt it was safe, waiting for when the nearest overseer had his attention on those in the field. Our conversation was brief. She told me she knew Matthias had received a similar lashing to mine but in the house, in front of the overseers.

His blood splattered on the walls, the floor, the furniture with each crack of the whip, then when the master was satisfied, "He made him clean it up, all of it, every drop," Rose sighed.

"His way of showing him the life he was giving up by choosing you, I suppose."

She shrugged when I asked what else would be done to him.

"He's let him go to his mother's house for the moment, but that's only out of his perverted sympathy for Zatia."

We both held to the hope that the lashing would be all the punishment he would receive and would be granted more grace than Asa had been given.

As the sun set, I could no longer feel my limbs, and my breath strained to sustain me. The wooden poles were rough and full of splinters, and the 'X' they were formed into bit into me as much as the rope that held me to it. My arms and legs were spread out along the shape, my nakedness on display for all to see as I hung there, a few inches from the ground.

I had held hope that I would be freed, but the truth that I might spend the night like this weakened me further. A light shone from the direction of the sleeping quarters and grew near. The sound of footsteps followed, and it was but a short time before I found Jasper looking at me, the torch illuminating his features.

"Thank you," I said, my words coming out in short puffs of strained air.

His severe expression dropped, eyes widened, and the blue in them shined in the darkness.

"I'm not here to free you."

He looked to his hand, clutching the handle of a small brown jug. The lip of its opening was chipped near the handle, and I could see the outline of its missing piece. I knew the jug immediately. It contained lamp oil. It was the very same vessel that Abel would use to refill in the lanterns in the stables.

Large flames burst up not too far from us, and I turned to find Asa's body engulfed in fire. It flowed up, licking at the rope and tree that supported him.

I understood then what I had refused to a moment ago.

"Please. Please, don't."

He shook his head with a heavy sigh.

"If I don't, I'll be right there burning with you."

"Then kill me first," I said. "Surely you can do that."

His expression was as still as carved stone.

"Lord Malcom ordered me not to, although I would if he weren't watching. I put in more than I was supposed to so it would go as quick as I could make it."

I caught a hint of pity as he looked at me, and I braced myself, closing my eyes. He saturated me, and I took a deep breath as he touched the flame to my feet.

Heat.

Pain beyond what feeble words could ever describe.

I heard myself cry out, scream in the distance.

Cold.

Wet.

I opened my eyes as the water splashed me. Drenched cloth struck me, covered me, fighting the blaze.

The shadow above me worked quickly. Arms handed him buckets, and he poured the water over me until there was no flame left.

I gasped, struggled to see my savior. He lifted me into his arms, holding me against him, and I knew him immediately.

Matthias.

Hands covered me with a soft cloth.

"The breaths she breathes are her last, son," Zatia said. "She will pass, and we will do what we can to make it as easy as possible, yes?"

Matthias trembled, and I felt despair in his breathing. I tried to speak, but my tongue could not form the words.

I clawed at him, *pleading* with him to hear me. I found him looking down at me, although I could see little.

"Ocean," I said. The last word I would be able to speak.

Zatia was right. My death was fast approaching.

The world darkened, even with my eyes open. I saw no stars, no moon, no sky, no night. Nothingness.

Matthias held me to him, and my body shuffled from time to time in his embrace. We were moving. I could hear the crack of a whip and the hooves of horses galloping. The clang of metal against rock. We were in a wagon.

After losing consciousness again, I found that we were now walking. Matthias, ever strong, still trembled, and I heard the ocean, the waves rolling in and slapping against the land.

The sound comforted me, and my heartbeat slowed, joining with the rhythm.

"We're here, Ia," he said, the first words I'd heard him speak. They were hoarse, weak.

"Ocean," I tried to say, finding nothing but garbled syllables.

"Put her in the water," Zatia said. "She might have a chance."

He stiffened, hesitated.

"I know you do not believe what I saw, but you must trust me. The salt water heals her. It may save her, and if nothing else, may ease her."

He moved, this time with more purpose, determination. The waves grew near, Calling to me, and I heard the spirit of my sister among them.

My skin tingled as he walked us farther in. My body floated, and the ocean pulled at me.

"Let her go, son," Zatia said as her hand caressed the top of my head. "Let the ocean take her."

Matthias lowered his lips, brushing them against me, and whispered with a cracking voice, "I love you, Ia. Thank you for loving me. I am sorry I failed you. *Forgive me.*"

His hold loosened, and the waves pulled at me. I floated, then with the remaining strength I had, I kicked away from him, pushing myself down into the depths and farther out into the sea.

f i f t e e n

THE PAIN THAT ENGULFED ME eased as I fought to swim farther down, but now I found myself struggling to breathe in the waters where I had been raised. Water burned in my lungs, and I choked, my limbs flailing, my body instinctively struggling to push to the surface – to air, to *life*.

The reality that I was dying ruptured through the calmness I struggled to keep.

The sensation was numbing yet tightening all at once, and my arms and hands drew to my chest, all of it involuntary, forceful. As my lips gasped for the air I had grown used to breathing, the world faded and turned still…and warm.

Time passed, and the water was dark when I opened my eyes. Nighttime. I could breathe, the burning fire in my chest and back had subsided. Movement of the gills behind my ears confirmed that I was not deceased.

My eyes adjusted, and I could see everything before me, unlike the weak vision I'd had as a human. My tail tensed and flexed beneath me as I regained my orientation. I pressed my hands to my face, my sides, my body.

Beautiful. Vain, yes, but it was true. No longer did I just have a strong will – I had the form to match.

Strong, powerful.

Vengeful.

Anger bubbled up faster than I could suppress it. *Malcom.*

I balled my hands into fists, and surfaced, keeping only my head above the water. I surveyed the shore before me, squinting to see if I could make out any forms. It was too dark. If he had been looking for me, the search likely ended. I called out a prayer for Matthias.

Malcom wouldn't dare kill him, his own son, would he? What would he do knowing his son had attempted to save a slave? The very one that he had been whipped mercilessly for? That was what I was, a slave, and there was no mistaking it. A Lesser on shore, and now, I would be swimming home to possibly find myself a Lesser there as well, and Ro waiting to own me.

Ro.

I would have to deal with him, no doubt. Bile bubbled up to my mouth with the mere thought of him.

Experience on shore, however, taught me that I was stronger than I realized. I would not be surprised in the least if I could even fight Ro – and not just with words. Fear exaggerates, and I no longer questioned my abilities, having replaced fear with the desperate need to save Matthias.

How could I do that? How could I save him from beneath the water?

I could try onshore, but with what success?

I needed a lure, a Caller, to help me, to bring into the water all who would do Matthias harm. Surely it could be done. My own voice was strong, but those of the practiced and successful – perhaps if they neared the shore, they could be loud enough in unison. It would be a risk with no guarantee that anyone would help me, but it would be worth a try.

Following the sights and scents, I began to make my way home. It would be quite a distance, but I would make it there by the time dawn broke. Elation flooded me, building alongside my anxiety. The longing to hug Mother and hold my sisters kept me focused on the good.

Liliana.

The last memory of her blurred and pained, a lifeless body plummeting with pieces of the vessels we were trying to conquer. I closed my eyes as a pain struck my heart, the reality of my loss no longer painted over by the overwhelming experience of turning human. There would be time to grieve. For now, I needed to make it home, to the family that loved me, to those who could *help me.*

TIME WAS SHORT, *THAT* I knew with dire certainty, but how did one ask for help from those who had probably assumed I was dead? I swam, rolling it over in my mind, too stressed and hurried to enjoy the familiar wave of my tail and the feel of water all around me, sliding against me as I propelled through the depths.

My gills flexed, my chest heaving for breath, yet I somehow seemed to be swimming faster than ever. All of the hobbling and toiling built my form stronger and sturdier than ever, and I was surprised to find that the strength could be found in my tail as well.

The waters turned lighter with the rising sun, and I found myself looking down over the formations that created our home. This time of morning, bodies would be bustling about, swimming from one area to the next, getting an early start on today's chores.

There was no one in sight.

No movement, no voices, nothing but the gentle float of seaweed that sprung up from the bottom. My heart fell. There would be no help here. The faces and embraces I had longed for were on their journey north, too far for me to catch up to them.

With a heavy heart, I made my way to the floor, winding through structures and passageways until I found the grotto my family lived in. Our meager belongings, some salvaged from ships, some made, still remained, and it confused me. Everything was laid out as if no one had left and would return at any moment. I picked up the shell Mother used to trim my hair, running my finger across the sharp edge.

My ears picked up a rustling, soft but near, behind me. I lowered the shell back to its place, preparing for whomever or whatever it was sneaking up.

I turned around as quickly as I could, and found the blades of a trident pushing into the skin at my neck. It was terrifying; Ro's trident – carefully crafted of coral and bone and incredibly sharp.

"Well, well, Ia," Ro said, his voice lilted with excitement and surprise. "I was expecting a thief, and here I find you returned from the dead."

"What are you doing here?" I was callous and cool, trying to hide the quickening beat of my heart.

"I believe I am the one in the most advantageous position to question." A slow smirk spread across his lips. "Where have you been?"

"You would not believe me," I said. "Where is my family, and what are you doing in here?"

He snorted, keeping the points of his weapon pressed to me.

"Liliana's mating ceremony, where everyone else is."

Liliana? My breath caught in my throat.

"She is alive? Unharmed?"

"Yes, and is enjoying the lavish rite brought by the High Mother."

Breath left me, and my body trembled in relief.

"Why are you not there? You are not the fortunate chosen, then?"

A soft laugh escaped him, and he drew himself closer to me.

"She found my younger brother to be a better match."

His lips kept their slimy smile, but his narrowed, darkening eyes betrayed him. He was furious, and here I was, yet another female who refused him at every turn. *Alone.*

He pushed me back, closing the distance between us. My arms reached behind me, feeling for the shelf, and a sharp breath escaped me as I sliced the tip of my finger on the shell I had just laid down. Thinking it was the pressure of the trident blades causing me pain, he snorted as he lowered his weapon.

"You need to leave," I said. "You are not welcome without escort in our home."

"I go where I please," he said. "It is my life I risk each time I defend our people, and I will enter wherever I choose. Where have *you* been?"

"Take me to the celebration, and I will tell everyone."

He shook his head.

"Not that simple. Everyone thinks you are a Forsaken, fleeing from your duties as a Lesser, even your own family."

"I am not a Lesser," I said. "I have had only one test."

"A bad one." He licked his bottom lip. "Or so the other Callers say. Volume, but no voice, just a shrill scream."

"That is none of your concern," I said, my temper rising to match my nervousness. "Get out of my way."

He stared at me for a moment, his brow furrowing.

"Your skin – it's darker."

I sighed, pushing away the trident with the palm of my free hand, the other poised behind me with the shell.

"You've been surfacing," he said, a sinister glow stretched across his face. "You know that is forbidden."

"I owe you no explanation. You will let me pass."

He leaned back.

"Of course. My apologies."

He waved his arm to the side, motioning for my exit. I kept my back to the wall, suspicious of his sudden release, saying nothing as I worked my way around him. The opening to our shelter was narrow, and his large form cramped the space, yet he did not budge, just continued to look down his nose at me, sneering, as I was forced up against him.

Squeezing past, I breathed a sigh of relief, thinking myself free of him for the moment until my head jerked back. He grabbed my short hair at the scalp, pulling me violently to him. Lashing out, I swung my hand containing the shell as I yanked myself free and turned to face him. A deep gouge formed across his left cheek, just under his eye, and his blood began to surface, dispensed by the water into tiny wisps of dark brown.

He tilted his head and thrust his throat against the edge of the shell, pressing into it until it broke the skin.

"You want to kill me? Here is your chance, but I shall warn you, if you do not, you will regret it the rest of your life."

A shudder tore through me, and my fear vanished as anger boiled up.

"So be it," I said, thrusting the edge into his neck.

Sensing my movement, he flenched as I pressed onward, his eyes wide in surprise, with a hint of terror, and he dodged out just out of my range. His mouth fell open as he regarded me, considered the fact that I was willing - and trying - to kill him.

"Do not ever think that I am not capable. Underestimating me will be your worst, and final, mistake."

My whole body shook with anxiety, and I remained poised to strike, keeping my focus on him, until I noticed that he was no longer looking at me, but behind me.

I lowered my makeshift weapon and turned to find my family, my tribe, and at the front of them all, the Caller of Honor, my sister – *Lilli*, and my mother. Their faces were full of shock. A low murmur rumbled among them.

"Ia," Mother whispered as she swam to me and wrapped her arms around me.

They talked among themselves as I embraced my family. Some of those muttering were confused to see me, others angry.

"You are not dead, Ia," Lili said, repeating it. "I thought you were dead."

"I worried the same for you, Lili," I answered.

"Where have you been?"

The voice came from behind me, angry and spiteful. Ro, of course.

"I found her stealing. A Forsaken trying to steal from her own family."

"I am not Forsaken, Ro," I said, shaking my head, appalled that he was twisting the situation to his favor – and my endangerment.

Faces darkened, and the expressions of those I love fell from relief to worry.

"Where have you been?" asked Mother, as softly as she could. "We found no trace of you, believed you to be no more."

"And what mermaid would leave her family to believe her to be dead? A Forsaken!"

Ro interjected before I had time to answer.

"I am not Forsaken! I have been ashore."

The words fell out. Truth was hard to contain, even when it could have meant my death. A roar of disbelief and growing anger tore loose among the people.

"Liar," someone shouted, and I looked back to Ro, now leaning against the entrance of my family's home with his arms crossed and a smug, horrible look on his face.

"I do not lie." I knew no one believed me, not even my own family, who were now looking away.

"Forsaken has trespassed – she must be punished," someone else yelled from the crowd, and shouts of "Yes!" and "Punish her!" supported it.

I cringed, looking around for an escape as I shook my head.

Several of the guards, Ro's friends, had managed to work their way to the front of the throng, pushing their way past my family. They looked to Ro, and with a nod of his head, they reached out to seize me.

"Stop!" An older and feminine voice called out. The crowd parted to reveal the High Mother. From the clay beads in her hair and the ceremonial necklace, she had been leading Liliana's mating rite. "You will do no such thing until I determine if she is truthful."

She swam through the middle of them at her leisure, stopping only a hand's width or two from me. I bowed to her, my thoughts flooding with an unspoken prayer that she would save me from Ro and his men. She reached out and took me by the chin, turning my head from side-to-side. Her brow furrowed, and she looked to Ro, her eyes narrowing at the sight of his wound.

"Come with me, child." She led me into the grotto, out of earshot from the others who respectfully kept their distance.

"Give me your hand," she said.

I offered my right hand, and she turned it over, running her long fingernails down the lines of my palm. Her mouth moved with whispers and the lines grew bright with a flash of light, then dissipated to nothing. She smiled, looking back up at me.

"You are, indeed, a land-strider," she said. "Of ocean and of ash. Mer and human, one and the same. My, I thought I should never see another one. I will have two hundred years on this aged frame with the next cycle of the moon."

She sighed as she continued.

"It is our blessing and our curse to have such long lives, Ia, especially compared to the humans."

I nodded as my breath caught in my throat, unsure where her comments were leading us.

"You were turned as an infant, so your lifespan will be eternal compared to his, and I sense you know this."

My mouth fell open. I had not thought about it, not once.

"If I should turn him? Would he be as our kind?"

She held up a finger. "If he survives, if you are successful, his life will still be shorter than yours. Longer than that of a human, but still but a fraction to yours."

Her eyes softened, and she caressed my chin. "The decision is all yours, Ia. Do you choose a life with him, or do you let it go?"

I shrugged. "Perhaps I am selfish, but I want to spend my life with him."

"Such is our curse, dear. We are given the gift to walk among them, and the smarter of us lure them to the water for our family to feast, but you," she said. "You have heart as I once did, Ia. One walks among them, then one grows to care for them, then one grows to love them – as you do him."

High Mother stared off for a moment, smiling in a memory.

"I fear he is in grave danger, and I do not know what to do."

The old woman threw back her head and laughed. "Go back ashore, lure this man who would harm you to the water, then take him to the depths and eat." She continued to laugh as she looked at me, my jaw slack, eyes wide, and eyebrows raised.

"High Mother, it took me too long to change forms, and I have no talent for Calling."

"Ha!" She waved. "Your talent for Calling will be in human form, and by the look of you, what a fierce one you will be. As for changing, *will* yourself to do it quickly, and it will happen. You could change into your human form right at this very moment if you wished."

I pursed as I determined to try, and my elder winked at me.

"One final piece of advice, girl," she said. "They believe you to be dead? Sing from the moment your feet touch the sand. Keep them in the dream your voice conjures until your deed is done. Your chosen will not be affected, nor will anyone you choose to spare."

"Yes, High Mother," I replied.

"Beware that young guard out there. Prove yourself truthful," she said as she turned to leave, clearing her throat. "And when the time is right, when you have done all you may, you and your family shall come to me, and I shall teach you."

She was vague, but I heeded her words and bowed as she stepped out, back among our people, and a tingle ran from my tail to the top of my head as I braced myself for the task at hand.

I would rescue Matthias.

s i x t e e n

THE NIGHT AIR BLEW AND chilled my head and face as I floated, looking to the shore. The whole of the tribe, save a chagrined young guard and a few of his companions, surfaced behind me and bobbed in silence, the High Mother among them. They would watch me change.

Calming my racing heart with a few deep breaths, I approached the shallow waters, the very ones that would strand a mermaid as they pulled her in toward land. There was very little room to move my tail, the tips of it already scraping against the ocean floor.

How does one will oneself to turn human?

I squeezed my eyes shut, repeating 'transform' as though magic were in the word. Nothing happened. Casting a look behind me, I could see slight movement among my supervisors, whispering with covered hands. This was taking too much time.

"You are thinking too much, Ia! Stop thinking and do," the High Mother yelled, drawing surprised looks from her flock who had been instructed from birth to keep silent when approaching the shore.

I bit my lower lip and let my body relax into the wave, the tip of my tail carving shapes in the sand. I stopped thinking of changing and started thinking of Matthias. Concern overwhelmed me, and I did my best to thrust it out with thoughts of us in the grass, his soft smile, the feel of the earth beneath me.

Earth beneath me. Beneath my *feet.*

Pain shot through me as my tail began to split. It was uncomfortable, as though I had ripped it with a sharp rock, but with the feeling came a familiar tingle that traveled up. I found myself flexing thighs, still covered in scales, and my tail gave way to legs, and then to feet.

I crunched my toes into the sand beneath them, smiling. Tiny bits of scale, iridescent in the moonlight, floated up around me, and I ran my hands down my form, finding only skin. Determination seized me, and I hobbled through the remainder of the shallow waters until all that was left were gentle waves lapping at my feet. Excited murmuring erupted from my group of voyeurs, which quickly gave way to cheering, despite the danger.

I waved at them, and then turned to gather my bearings. Walking without the help of a broom or my cane was challenging, but concern for Matthias quickened my feet.

As I approached the top of the short ridge where the land turned from sand into grass and brush, I made out Zatia's home in the dark, my eyes now fully human and limited. No light or sign of occupation could be seen, and as I neared, I heard the High Mother's voice on the wind, Calling me to sing.

My voice rang out in the dark, and it was not the shrill, horrendous sound I had made all those nights ago at my first

Calling as a mermaid. The tone of it was now melodious, rich, and I called for the wary to rest, to slumber.

Excitement and hope ran up my body. My song permeated the night, and I continued past Zatia's home and down the path I had first traveled a lifetime ago in the back of a wagon.

The breeze blew from the direction of my people, carrying my voice on the wind, amplifying my song as morning broke across the horizon. Slaves beginning their daily labor in the fields stopped and considered me for a moment before their lids grew heavy, and they laid themselves down. The overseers did so as well, some crawling away from me in failed attempt to pull themselves out of earshot before sleep claimed them.

My time would be limited before I would need to sing them back into slumber. Melina Hills stretched out before me, the house shadowed by the hills surrounding it. The expanse of fields between myself and my destination were Matthias' usual domain, but I only caught sight of Jasper, the man who had beaten Joseph within an inch of his life.

He was atop Matthias' favored soft brown mare and sought to spur her away when he saw me after watching all those around him collapse to the ground. I smiled as I sang, keeping the song of rest on my lips as I tightened my throat, forcing out a trail of different pitches until my voice carried the song of luring as well. Jarring at first, I found the sounds merging naturally as I had heard Lili do in practice. Jasper's eyes widened as his thoughts receded into nothing but my will, and he guided his horse to me.

With a gentle lift, he helped me up and guided us along until the great manor loomed over us. My lips, were dry and cracking - my throat pained by the time we reached the back of the house, and we dismounted. I stopped singing, and with my hand balled up into a fist, I struck Jasper in the face, knocking him back.

"Where is Matthias?"

He shook his head, tossing out the limbo his mind had been trapped in as he reached up to his nose, smearing blood across his face.

"Slave quarters," he said, and as soon as I hummed the first note, he fell to the ground, splayed out as he slept.

MATTHIAS, CHAINED TO THE WALL in a dark corner, was beyond recognition. One eye was swollen shut, and dried blood covered him. His right arm dangled in an unnatural, gruesome position, and his breathing was rapid and shallow.

Zatia was asleep next to him with a basket of blood-soaked herbs, and I bent over to shake her awake. Her eyelids cracked open as she jerked away from me, terrified. I stepped into a crack of light, and she cried out as she recognized me, lunging to hug me.

"They will hang him tonight," she pleaded. "We must do something!"

I nodded, handing her the keys that I had pulled off Jasper's unconscious person.

"Will he live?" Tears welled up and blurred my vision.

"I pray so," she said. "Jiba can help me heal him, but she will not come here for fear that Lord Malcom will take her daughter from her again."

"Take him to your home," I said, bending down to kiss his forehead.

He lifted his head, bloodied lips forming a smile.

"Are you here to take my soul?"

"No," I said, smiling. "I am here to take Lord Malcom's."

I FOUND THE MASTER STILL snoring, fast asleep despite the morning light pouring in through the windows, so it was with little effort that I was able to lure him to his feet, down the stairs, through the foyer, and on until we reached the gates.

Jasper, too, followed with the same wide-eyed, blank stare and soft mumbling as I sang to them of their deepest desires, of the treasure and beauty that awaited them in the depths. Each field we passed, I called to the slumbering overseer until I had each in a neat line trailing behind me.

It took some time to reach the shore. A broomstick steadied me, but my pace was still slow. I walked backward to keep my eye upon my captives, knowing that if I for one second failed, they would come to their senses. I did not even cast a glance to Zatia's home when we came near, scared that sorrowful news could await me.

When we stepped into the water, I heard Mother's voice, then Liliana's – both Calling the men that were following in, buying me time to complete the transformation. The men swam around me as though I did not exist, and it was a short time later that I heard the song cease, the call complete, and the men devoured.

Except one.

Lord Malcom stood within the water to his knees staring out into the expanse, the spell of the song breaking. His brow was furrowed, his gaze searching. He appeared confused and worried.

"Strange," I thought aloud. "Why does he not swim out to the song?"

He tried to step forward, knowing it was the direction he should go, but stopped short upon seeing the water. I could make out a form running toward us.

"He will not go in," Zatia yelled out, her voice jerking Lord Malcom's attention to her. "His fear is far stronger than his desire. He is terrified of water. *He cannot swim.*"

A light sparked in Lord Malcom's eyes. His expression relaxed, then grew resolute as his jaw tensed. A sense of awareness flooded his face. He was awake and furious. Unintelligible words, curses and shouts tore through his lips, and then he turned to run to Zatia. My tail was only half-formed, but I pushed on the tips of my fins with all my might and reached for him, just catching his shoulder. My fingernails, sharp and pointed as my teeth, dug in to his flesh, and he shouted in pain, thrashing his way out of the water with me now attached to his back.

Yelling, he swung to knock me off his back, but I held fast, pulling myself against him. He was strong, and I would not be able to hold for long.

My lower jaw unhinged as I opened my mouth wide as my transitioning form would let me, and I sunk my teeth into the side of his neck. Blood spurted forth, sweet and warm, and I found myself renewed by the taste of his flesh as I bit down and ripped.

He jolted, throwing me across his shoulder and down to the beach. Towering over me, he stood clutching his neck. My wound had been devastating but not yet fatal. The look in his eyes told me he knew, understood, that this was a fight to the death.

I kicked and thrashed my half-formed legs, trying to push myself away from him. His eyes searched all around us, coming to rest on a large rock next to me. With a single motion, he swooped down and grabbed it with his free hand, bringing it up to strike me.

I had not the leverage nor the buoyance to leap for him, despite the tide rising around us.

He straddled me, pressing his foot down on my left knee as he lowered himself to bludgeon me.

Thin, brown leather wrapped around his neck with a loud crack, startling me. Matthias was standing to my right, his bruised arm tightening the whip, groaning in pain as he pulled Lord Malcom to his knees.

Malcom gasped for air, his hands grabbing at the leather, fighting against its pull. With but a short distance between them, Matthias let loose the whip and dove for his father, knocking him back.

Matthias squeezed his remaining strong hand around Malcom's throat and screamed, shaking as he lifted Malcom by the neck with a single hand. Sobs tore from Matthias as the man began to tremble, his life leaving him, and Matthias let him go, dropping him to the ground. Malcom convulsed, each spasm shorter than the last as his life began to leave him. His throat was nearly crushed and blood from my bite was seeping out in an increasing amount.

My legs now formed, I embraced Matthias as he cried into my hair. With Zatia's help, we staggered toward her home as the waves began to pull Lord Malcom's lifeless body.

Epilogue

Standing on the balcony off our bedroom, overlooking the gate of Melina Hills, I took in the warmth of the newly breaking dawn, rubbing my swollen belly and softly humming the songs of the seas to the growing life inside me.

I had foreseen our first girl in my dreams, much to my excitement after our boy, who I could already hear running around outside below me.

Matthias' soft touch on my shoulder startled me, and I jumped, laughing as he wrapped his arms around me, kissing my neck, smelling my hair.

"You, dear husband, are supposed to be working," I said, smiling as I savored his affection.

"You, beautiful wife, were too appealing for me to walk past," he said, whispering against my skin. "Besides, doing things as I please comes with my position. Helps ease the stress of responsibility."

I could feel him smile against me as he placed a hand on my belly.

"Seven years, and we finally have a home I am happy to welcome our children into," he said with a sigh of relief.

All was right in the world, or at least in our part. Malcom's death had been investigated, albeit poorly, and it was judged from his consistent abuse of alcohol that he likely wandered into the ocean and drowned.

As for the overseers, Matthias claimed they'd all been thieves who took the first boat they could after the master's death. He paid a ship captain a lovely sum of gold kept in Lord Malcom's desk to list their names on his register of passengers.

After a year of debate, Matthias was granted the estate and all its holdings as per Lord Malcom's unaltered will – without the title of Lord, which was awarded to Lord Malcom's brother's family, much to Matthias' pleasure.

Matthias' first act as owner was to free all those laboring there, and to offer wages and decent shelter to those who would stay to tend to the crops. Some left and returned, some left never to be seen again, and others stayed, surprised to find Matthias working among them as their homes were built.

Pieces of the outlying pastures were sold to fund our vision of Melina Hills, although we found ourselves blessed shortly thereafter with an incredibly lucrative sale of Lord Malcom's horses, allowing us to buy the lands back and free as many slaves as we could purchase at the market, much to the chagrin of our slave-holding neighbors.

I was beside him for it all as he made his penance, burying the shame of his past and his father with each passing day. From time to time, my body would call to me, and I would visit the ocean, wrapping myself in its waves, feeling the freedom of the water as our children ran along the beach.

I was home either way – on land or in the water, and the peace I had was unsurpassable. After all, I was of ocean and ash, and I had finally discovered that while I belonged *to* neither world, I belonged *in* both.

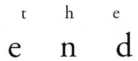

a c k n o w l e d g m e n t s

Mom, Josh, and Logan – Book Number Two! Yay! There's no way I could do any of this writing stuff without you. Words could never express how much I love you.

Anna Albergucci and Bokerah Brumley – Thank you for holding my hand through this one. I would not be doing this without you ladies either.

B.I.C. Writers Group – Thank you for allowing me to join you! Your advice and encouragement is worth more than all the gold and webinars in the world. Thank you!

To all my family and friends who have shown me such love and support along the way – Thank you!

To God and Jesus – Thank you for keeping me semi-sane!

To my editor, Allison, The Write Conclusion, who did an incredible job working with me on this – Thank you! If this story is in any way good, it's thanks to your sharp eye.

To my formatter, Nadege with Inkstain Interior Book Design – Thank you! Your patience is positively angelic. Thank you for squeezing this in and doing such an awesome job.

To Staci Brillhart, quirky-bird.com, for yet another gorgeous cover – Thank you! You are amazing! <3

To anyone that I may have forgotten – Thank you!...and I'm sorry if I didn't mention you by name. There will be other books... Lord willing.

With Love,
Amber (A.R.) Draeger

A.R. (Amber) Draeger resides in rural Texas with her husband, Josh, and their son, Logan. *Daughters of Men* is her debut horror/thriller/sci-fi novella. *Of Ocean and Ash* is her debut romance novella.

www.amberdraeger.com
www.facebook.com/ardraeger
www.twitter.com/adraeger

ABOUT THE FALLING IN DEEP COLLECTION:
Coming summer 2015

From mermaids to sirens, Miami to Athens, dark paranormal
romance to contemporary stories with steam, the fifteen
award-winning and best-selling authors of the Falling
in Deep collection are bringing you mermaid tales
like you've never seen before.

Every week beginning June 1st, 2015, we'll be releasing one
unique, never-before-published novella! Each novella will
feature our favorite creature of the deep.

NOW ENJOY A SNEAK PEEK FROM:

Deep Breath by J.M. Miller
Coming soon...

Before disappearing at sea, Marissa Pruitt's father—a once
revered marine archaeologist—walked the line of insanity,
claiming to have seen a mermaid during an ordinary dive in
the Gulf of Mexico. He abandoned his life and career,
completely obsessed with chasing the truth.

It's been years since his death, and Marissa is still tormented
by countless unanswered questions. When she finds dive
coordinates and a stone pendant hidden in her father's things,
she asks for help from his old protégé and sets out to give her
father one last goodbye and maybe find closure for her
troubled heart. Instead, she finds the truth he'd been
searching for all along, with a life and love she never could
have imagined. But there's a price to see it all, one set by
betrayal and paid with an anchor at her feet
and salt water in her lungs.

1

A drop of rain smacked the necklace Marissa held in her palm, splattering against the dark green stone and the threaded knots that encased it like a fishing net. She wiped a finger over the pendant and glanced down past her hands to the waves below. The gulf's swells had grown while she'd been lost in her thoughts. They were no longer calm, no longer in sync, rocking and slapping her rental boat for disrupting their chaotic rhythm. Reflections of lightning flashed across the waves' peaks and the rumble of thunder quickly followed. Marissa looked up toward the open water horizon as thick gray clouds rolled in like a slow motion avalanche, threatening to bury the setting sun. She wasn't concerned so much with the storm, only that Darci was well over an hour late. With darkness and strong currents approaching, the dive she had planned was out of the question. It would have to wait for another day.

Marissa looked at the necklace again. Swirled with colors much like those the Emerald Coast was known for, the rough stone was gorgeous. She couldn't comprehend why her father had kept it inside a box of old photos, but then again, she'd never understood the reasons for most of his actions leading up to his disappearance six years before. No one had. He'd been crazed, obsessed with what he claimed to have seen on a typical dive in the Gulf of Mexico. It had cost him his career, recognition as one of the most notable marine archaeologists in the state of Florida, many friends and colleagues, most of his savings, and in the end, his life.

His body was never found.

The confusion of it all had made a teenage Marissa doubt him as well, and it had troubled her over the years, never knowing the reason her father had turned from renown to reckless. It was the reason she'd rented the boat, to give him one last chance. Maybe he had seen something. Was it a mermaid as he'd claimed? Probably not, but maybe there was an explanation.

Following another cluster of lightning cracks, the sound of an approaching motor caught her attention. She tucked the necklace into the pocket of her windbreaker and moved around the center console to the back of the boat, watching a white cruiser with a hard top pull closer as a few more raindrops fell. It throttled down, and a woman wearing an aqua colored dress shirt and black suit skirt stepped out of the cabin's door. Her short brown hair held loose curls that fluttered as the wind swept between the two boats.

"Marissa. It's wonderful to see you again. Sorry I'm late," Darci said, walking the length of the cruiser and tossing fenders over the side so the boats could raft up.

"It's no problem at all, Darci. Thanks for coming," Marissa responded, catching the lines Darci pitched across to tie off.

Darci ducked back inside the cabin to ease the boats together, then cut off the cruiser's motor and stepped back outside onto the rear swimming platform, barefooted. "Nice rental. Gear too?" She nodded her head toward the tanks and vests then rolled up her sleeves and boarded the rental boat. "Now I know why you declined my dinner invitation in Pensacola and requested to meet on the water." Her arms opened for an embrace. "Feeling a bit nostalgic?"

Marissa opened her arms and leaned closer, accepting the hug awkwardly. After all, it was a bit odd. Sure Darci Barington had been her father's protégé at the state's historical resources department for several years, learning intricacies about underwater excavation and retrieval from one of the best in the field, but Marissa could count the number of times they'd conversed on two hands. Even those had barely passed beyond a simple greeting. Darci was just one of those people who looked to have a lot more brewing below her outer facade. It was a feeling Marissa couldn't shake.

She backed up to a more comfortable distance and nodded, eying Darci with a friendly smile. The years had changed Darci in a fair amount of ways. The skin around her gray eyes showed thin lines from the trials of life, but it made them look sharp instead of tired, like she'd grown accustomed to studying people more keenly.

Not waiting for a reply, Darci said, "Sorry I was unable to speak longer on the phone earlier this morning, but things have been busy in the private sector. That's also why I couldn't attend your mother's funeral. I was very saddened to hear of her passing."

Marissa shook her head lightly as memories of her mother's battle with cancer flashed to mind. That battle had ended the month prior, offering more relief than grief. Her mother had finally found peace. "I definitely understand. Thank you for sending flowers. They were beautiful."

"As was your mother. She was strong and priceless, Nick's real treasure."

Marissa bit her bottom lip with a nod, knowing her father had never found the peace her mother had in death. Even though Nick had been content with his family, the urge to find his truth had consumed him. More rain tapped on Marissa's windbreaker, snapping her thoughts back. "Congratulations on the start of your own company. I can see leaving the state job has been a good move for you." She glanced at the cruiser.

Darci shifted her stance wider as the waves rocked the boats and ran a palm across her forehead, wiping away a few drops of rain. "Thank you. I'm still based here in Florida, but I bounce around along the gulf and sometimes abroad. Far too much of it all is spent above the water, regrettably." She grinned, flashing a quick, endearing wrinkle in her nose.

Marissa remembered her father saying how eager Darci had been when she'd first started working with him, never wanting to leave the water, always looking for the next find. Her passion had rivaled his own, which was exactly why he'd hired her.

Darci's small grin disappeared, considering Marissa's silence. "But you certainly didn't travel all the way from Dallas to float out here and chat with me about my job. I take it you found something in your parents' old place worth calling me out here for."

"I apologize for taking up your time, and I definitely don't want to waste it, but I thought out of anyone he used to associate with, you'd be the one who'd at least entertain my curiosity."

The sides of Darci's bright red lips lifted the tiniest bit and she turned toward the open water. "The Chevron artificial reef is just south of here. The USS Oriskany, too. Your father and I dove these waters countless times. He taught me so much." She fell silent for a moment. Drops of rain tapped the boats faster as the clouds continued to steal the daylight. Darci glanced over her shoulder at Marissa. "I kept looking for him, you know? Even after they found the boat. I'm just sorry there wasn't more I could do for him. If there had been, things might have been different."

Marissa sighed. "I feel the same regret. He deserved much more from me, though. I was his daughter, and I brushed him aside like everyone else. I should have supported him no matter how crazy I thought …" She shoved her hands into her windbreaker pockets, one hand clenching the necklace's pendant, the other clenching the cloth she'd found it wrapped in.

"Don't be too hard on yourself. You were starting college, starting your own life. I'm sure he understood that. He just wasn't making much sense then. He was paranoid and distant, and when he started talking about mermaids … things just went downhill." Darci ran her fingers through her dampened hair. "Look, it's not a good idea to dive in this storm. Let's step inside my cabin and you can tell me what this is about. Then maybe we can go have that dinner."

Marissa clenched the necklace one more time, worried, unsure of what she needed to do. Her father wasn't one to hide things. There had to be a reason, but she would need help if she really wanted to find an answer. Darci was her only hope. Unfazed by the rain pelting her head and face harder, she yanked the pendant from her pocket and grabbed Darci's arm before she could step over to the cruiser. "This," she said, stretching her palm out close to Darci's face. "This is what I found. A necklace, stashed inside a box of old pictures, wrapped in a cloth. The cloth is why we're out here." Marissa grabbed the cloth from her other pocket and held it up beside the pendant. The DMS coordinates 30°09'46.3"N 87°00'42.5"W were written in marker on the beige cloth.

Darci's eyes widened and her lips parted. With soft fingers, she touched both the pendant and the cloth. "Nick never noted coordinates for personal stuff."

"No," Marissa confirmed. "He found more pleasure in dead reckoning, exploring without charts. He knew this area well enough to get around without them. That's why I knew it had to be important. This could just be a starting point, but at least it's a start."

Darci's eyes never left Marissa's palms. "It's definitely his writing." The words trailed off into a whisper, drowned out easily by the patter of rain. She leaned closer to study the pendant. "He never mentioned finding a stone, and he always logged his work data. Why would he do this?"

"It has to be connected to what he was looking for," Marissa stated as Darci lifted the necklace from her palm. "I mean, I'm not saying that mermaids are real, but maybe he saw something down there that he couldn't explain despite all his years diving. He was a focused man, Darci. You know that as well as I do. What if he was telling the truth? What if he found something?" Marissa leaned over the side of the boat, staring down at the water, wondering what he could have seen.

"Oh, this is definitely something." Darci dangled the pendant between her fingers and glanced past it to Marissa. "Did you mention this to anyone else?"

"No, just you. I didn't think anyone else would even bother with me."

Darci's eyes darted back to the stone. "I knew he'd been hiding something. The mermaid thing just seemed far-fetched. He must have found an undocumented wreck. If this is what came from it, we need to keep this between—"

A bigger wave crashed against the far side of the boat, knocking both women off balance. As Darci tried to recover, the necklace flew from her grasp, over the side of the boat. Both women gasped in horror and scrambled to catch it as it sailed toward the water.

For Marissa, there was no hesitation, no delay. She dropped the cloth and dove overboard without concern. Her phone, her clothes—none of it mattered. This was her father's life's work, something she could possibly use to right his name.

It was her only chance to find his truth. Without it, she would never really know what happened, why he'd disappeared those years ago.

With her arms fully extended, eyes focused on the pendant and its nylon cord trailing behind, she stretched her fingers and grazed its edge before closing her eyes and plunging into the ocean. The warmth of the salt water cocooned her, erasing the chill from the rain and wind above. Feeling the pendant in her palm, she squeezed her fingers closed, digging her nails into her flesh to the point of pain. There was no way she'd risk letting go. She mentally promised her father as much, feeling closer to him than she had in a very long time.

Marissa spun beneath the water and kicked back to the surface, breaking through the waves and opening her eyes to the stormy sky once again.

"Did you get it?" Darci yelled as lightning marbled the gray clouds above the boats.

Keeping her fist clenched, Marissa lifted her hand above the water. The cord dangled to her wrist, but the stone was still safely imprisoned by her fingers. "Yeah, I got it!"

"Excellent." Darci tipped her chin up and ran her hands back through her soaking hair, inhaling a relieved breath.

The roar of thunder ripped through the air, making Marissa kick more urgently toward the boat. Darci dropped the ladder and grabbed the wrist of Marissa's clenched hand to help her aboard. "Sorry about that. I'm glad you have quick reflexes."

"I am too." Marissa stepped around the air tanks and glanced back at Darci, noticing Darci's eyes were fixed on her clenched hand. She lifted her fist and immediately realized why: her hand was glowing. Light peeked through the cracks between her fingers. It wasn't very bright, just visible enough to see in the dullness of the stormy day. Slowly, she twisted her wrist and lifted each finger, revealing the stone pendant.

The thin white swirls inside the green stone flickered. Marissa gaped at the light, confusion and wonder rendering her speechless. How was it even possible? Fat raindrops continued to fall, and after several hit the necklace, the light began to fade.

"That's definitely not jade," Darci murmured as she moved closer.

Marissa cradled the necklace between her hands and pulled it in toward her body. Her hair dripped more water onto the stone, but this time instead of fading, the light within the swirls glinted, like tiny little flares bursting inside. "What the ..." Marissa lifted her hands closer to her face.

After a few more drops, Darci's eyes lit up as bright as the stone. "It's the water." She snatched the pendant from Marissa's hands, spun around, and ducked toward the back of the boat.

"No!" Marissa lunged toward her.

"I won't drop it," Darci reassured, weaving the nylon cord through fingers on both hands as she bent toward the waves. "Didn't you see it? The rain was dousing it, but the salt water from your hair ... it was almost igniting it. Look!" she yelled over her shoulder as another crash of thunder boomed overhead.

A wave engulfed Darci's hands and the stone flashed, lighting up the water around her skin with a soft halo.

"What is it?" Marissa asked. It was gorgeous, but it was like nothing she'd ever seen. Not in any textbooks or scientific studies. Not in any museum. Not from her father. She would have surely remembered something so marvelous.

Darci cupped water in her hands to keep the stone submerged then stood back up. Her head shook the slightest bit. "I ... I honestly don't know. I would guess it's biological, some kind of microorganism living inside the porous stone— well, that's what I'd guess if we'd just found it on a dive. But, since you said it's been sitting in a box in your parents' house,

I'm not sure how that would be possible." She shook her head again.

Marissa peeled her windbreaker over her head and dropped it in a soggy heap at her bare feet. Her phone spilled out of the pocket with a thud. Dead. There was no hope for it now. She squeezed some excess water from her shorts and tank top as she looked up to the sky, allowing the rain to massage her face with its unrelenting assault, considering the next step. As much as she wanted answers, she would have to wait. The storm was only getting worse. "We shouldn't stay out here much longer. Maybe we can research things tonight then come back to dive tomorrow if you aren't busy and if the weather cooperates." She moved closer, watching the last bit of salt water trickle through Darci's fingers.

With water streaming down her face, hair plastered to her cheeks, Darci finally tore her eyes from the dimming stone to acknowledge Marissa. "Yeah ... that sounds like a good idea. I'll clear everything I have tomorrow."

Marissa smiled and lifted her hand to take the necklace, noticing Darci's body react by shifting backward and dropping her hands a tad. It was as if she wasn't willing to let it go. Marissa narrowed her eyes. "Something wrong?"

"No, sorry." The edges of Darci's lips quirked up and a few lines wrinkled her nose. "Work habits. Whenever I'm on the water, I'm usually the lead." She tipped the necklace over, letting it dangle over Marissa's palm.

Darci's explanation was understandable, but Marissa couldn't stifle a pang of doubt creeping up the back of her neck. She smiled anyway and reached up to take the necklace. Just as her fingers closed around the pendant, Darci's body shifted again and her other fist smashed into Marissa's cheek.

Marissa screamed as her body spun from the impact. Shaken and stunned from the hit, she staggered forward toward the dive gear. There was no time to shield her face before colliding with a tank. Everything disappeared with a flash.

MARISSA WINCED AS A RUSH of sensations awakened. Her forehead throbbed, pulsing a sharp pain outward, wrapping around her skull and traveling down her neck. Raindrops tapped all over her face, stinging a spot above her brow with each hit. There had to be a cut or gash there. She cracked her eyes open to the clouds above. They had taken over most of the sky with a shade of gray closer to black than white. Lightning ripped through them, making them flash like the pendant.

Darci, Marissa thought, remembering what had happened. How long had she been lying there?

She lifted her head just as Darci stepped back onto the rental boat from the cruiser. "Darci? What the hell?" When she attempted to move her feet, she heard the rattle of chain and felt its cool metal weighing on her bare ankles.

Darci didn't look at her. "After all the years your father and I dove together, all the work we'd done, I knew he hadn't just lost his mind. Like everyone else, I believed it possible for a mind to snap under heavy frustration, but I knew he was too composed for that to happen. Even when I confronted him, though, he refused to tell me the truth." Darci lifted an anchor and positioned it at the back of the boat, moving a chain with it. "So thanks for contacting me. I'm sure I'll be able to find whatever he was searching for a little easier now." She patted her chest where the necklace hung.

"Don't do this, Darci," Marissa pleaded, realizing this wasn't some petty disagreement that had accidentally escalated. It was dire, and it was intentional.

Darci glanced down. The lines around her eyes softened a moment, then she heaved the anchor and thick chain overboard.

Marissa shrieked when the slack ran out and yanked hard at her ankles. Darci grabbed the chain and dragged her body closer to the edge of the boat. Realizing what was about to happen, Marissa thrashed her arms and legs, trying to stop her movement. She hooked the tank separators, causing the tanks to clank together and fall over, spreading the rest of the gear across the deck.

"Darci, don't!" Shock and desperation left her mouth through a strangled cry. "I don't care about what's down there. You can have it."

"I know I can. I'll most certainly find it, but that's no longer your concern. Bye Marissa. Tell your father I said thanks." She picked up the chains closer to Marissa's feet, yanked one more time, then stepped out of Marissa's reach.

Marissa tried to grab hold of anything that would help, only to slip past most of the gear. As she felt her feet leave the boat, she snagged a handheld bailout bottle of back-up air with an on-demand mouth regulator. Her other hand locked onto the edge of the boat, stopping her body from submerging. Even though it seemed like the end, she refused to give up.

Darci wasted no time. She moved closer and attempted to stomp Marissa's hand. Marissa moved her hand to avoid the hit and latched onto Darci's ankle, hoping to gain some leverage despite the heavy weight pulling her body down. She also swung the bailout bottle, hitting Darci's leg repeatedly. Darci lurched away, stumbling and falling back onto the deck. More hope ran through Marissa as she dug her nails into Darci's flesh, but it was short-lived. Darci drew her other foot back then slammed it into Marissa's head, breaking her hold and knocking her into the ocean.

Marissa gasped for one last breath and shoved the bailout bottle's regulator into her mouth as her face went under.

Made in the USA
Charleston, SC
14 June 2015